W9-ACM-226

TEKWAR

TEKWAR

WILLIAM SHATNER

AN ACE/PUTNAM BOOK
PUBLISHED BY G. P. PUTNAM'S SONS
NEW YORK

An Ace/Putnam Book
Published by G. P. Putnam's Sons
Publishers Since 1838
200 Madison Avenue
New York, NY 10016

Published simultaneously in Canada

A limited first edition of this book
has been published by Phantasia Press.

Library of Congress Cataloging-in-Publication Data

Shatner, William.
TekWar / William Shatner.
p. cm.
I. Title.
PS3569.H347T45 1989 89-10156 CIP
813'.54—dc20
ISBN 0-399-13495-6

Printed in the United States of America
1 2 3 4 5 6 7 8 9 10

This work is dedicated to those friends and colleagues from "Star Trek" and "T. J. Hooker," whose talents have contributed in no small measure to whatever successes I have achieved.

Acknowledgments

Writing a book is both an agony and an ecstasy. Wrestling with an empty page and a barren brain is the agony. Putting a period on the last sentence of a well-constructed paragraph is the ecstasy. Between the two lies the abyss of the novel. In order to cross that crevasse, I needed help.

Ron Goulart, a wonderful writer, showed me the way out and showed me the way in to completing the novel. He did an enormous amount of work and I shall be grateful to him for a long time to come.

In addition, I'd like to express my gratitude to Susan Allison, Roger Cooper and Chris Schillig at G. P. Putnam's for their help.

Acknowledgment should also be extended to my agents, Ivy Fisher Stone and Fifi Oscard in New York; and to my good friend and agent from that organization, Carmen LaVia, for his dedication and know-how in making this idea become a reality.

TEKWAR

1

He didn't know he was about to come back to life.

Up in the orbiting penal colony he slept, unaware of anything. Time had passed, days and weeks and then months and years, and he kept sleeping that long sleep. Suspended in a coffinlike plastic cubicle in the great orbiting prison that passed endlessly around the Earth, passing over Greater Los Angeles again and again.

Today that was all going to change, but Jake Cardigan didn't know anything about it. Not yet.

The gleaming, broad-shouldered robot was wearing a spotless white suit, and his chrome face and skull were freshly polished. He came striding purposefully through the crowds of wayfarers on the clear-plas colored ramps that interlaced within the vast seethru domes of the Greater Los Angeles Spaceport.

It was a hot, hazy morning in the spring of the year 2120 and the sectors of GLA that rose up around the port already had a blurred, sooty-orange hue. The fuzzy sky was full of motion. Aircabs, skycruisers, airvans and skybuses all flickered through the blur, sleek monorail trains went whizzing silently by at a dozen different levels, and both the crisscrossing pedestrian ramps and the sharply curving motorways were crowded. All the drone and roar of it was kept out of the domes of the spaceport.

A sudden barking broke out two ramps above the hurrying robot. One of the small mechanical sensor-dogs had spotted some sort of smuggler, a slim dark young man, and started to chase him. They went zigzagging along a green-tinted ramp right overhead, toppling some travelers and leaving assorted sounds of surprise and outrage in their wake.

The robot ignored the chase, pushing his way around the spacetourists who'd paused to gaze upward and rubberneck.

A skinny ten-year-old Japanese boy, just home from a Moon camp according to his pullover shirt, bumped into the white-suited robot and steadied himself with candy-smudged fingers.

The robot lifted him out of his way with both chrome hands, then brushed the small sticky smears from his breast pocket.

Gradually the crowds thinned and the colors of the walls and ramps dimmed and eventually everything was gray and the robot was in a less frequented section of the port. A human porter, a fake-legged veteran of the Brazil Wars, recognized the robot as they passed each other on a gray ramp. "Going up to the Freezer again, huh?"

"Obviously," answered the mechanical man in his deep metallic voice.

"Hell of a place to visit."

"Yet better to visit it than remain there."

"Yeah, I guess." The porter gave a shivering shrug, got a fresh grip on the handle of the luggage cart he was guiding and continued on.

The access door the robot wanted had a pale green light screen suspended over it. The screen blanked as the white-suited robot approached. Then words appeared—SHUTTLE FLIGHT 16 TO PENAL COLONY NOW READY FOR BOARDING. ALL PRISONERS SAFELY LOADED. NO DANGER TO PASSENGERS.

The robot brushed again at the place where the boy had touched him, made a sound in his metal throat that resembled, slightly, a laugh. Spreading the chrome palm of his left hand open wide, he touched the thumb with his right forefinger. The palm hummed faintly for exactly four seconds, then a slip of bright yellow paper came whirring out of a thin slot in his hand.

Jerking it free, the robot handed it to the gray-uniformed young woman who'd appeared in the open access doorway.

She took the special ticket a bit gingerly, scanned it. "Oh, you're Winger (M6)/SCPS-31PB," she said, checking his name off the short passenger list.

"We met on a shuttle flight up to the Freezer just eleven months ago," he reminded her. "You ought to make a better effort to memorize passengers. Especially those who work for the Southern California Parole Authority."

The shuttle attendant said, "Yes, I should've remembered the suit."

Winger brushed at his coat yet again. "If you'll stand aside," he suggested, "I'll see about getting aboard."

She pushed herself back against the wall, gesturing him into the boarding tunnel.

The prisonbound shuttle roared and vibrated as it went climbing up through the blurred orange morning and away from Greater Los Angeles.

Winger recrossed his metal legs and glanced casually around the gray cabin. There were only three other passengers sharing this section with him. All going up to visit prisoners, judging from the forlorn look of them. "Very one-sided experience," he remarked to himself inside his metal skull.

Back in the rear section, safely locked behind a dirt-smeared sheet of tough plastiglass, sat five new prisoners heading up to the Freezer. Among them were a cyborg veteran of the Brazil Wars who'd been rated an incurable thief and sentenced to fifty years in suspended animation; a lank black man convicted of smuggling the illegal electronic brain stimulant called Tek and given a twenty-five-year sentence; a twice-convicted Hispanic rapist set to do five years; a plump thirty-one-year-old blonde woman convicted of unlicensed prostitution and given four years; a youthful telekinetic thief arrested for a series of shopliftings at the Malibu Sector Underwater Mall and sentenced to seven.

Winger had data on the whole lot, but none of them especially interested him. Making that sound that wasn't exactly a laugh, he turned away from the prisoners.

One of the visitors had brushed against Winger as they were disembarking and gotten tears and some sort of magenta eyelid stain on the right sleeve of his coat. He was still rubbing at it as he entered the A–C section of the Administration Offices of the prison colony.

He walked rapidly across the gray, ribbed flooring to the large half-circle gunmetal desk at the oval room's center. He seated himself in the steel visitors' chair and waited, drumming chrome fingers on both chair arms, while the recog camera that was mounted on the desk looked him over.

"Winger (M6)/SCPS-30 PB," said the desk's voxbox after he'd been recognized. "What can we do for—"

"My name is Winger (M6)/SCPS-*31* PB," he corrected as he unzipped his jacket and then unzipped his paisley shirt.

"Noted. And what can we do for you today?"

"I have a Special Parole Release order plus all the standard Parole Forms required." He touched three spots on his bare chrome chest and forms of various shades and shapes started whirring out of a thin slot. When he had the sufficient amount, the robot spread them out atop the desk and closed his shirt and coat. "I'm requesting the release of Prisoner #19,587: Cardigan, Jake."

The recog camera read the assortment of official forms, voxbox muttering slightly. "All seem to be in order."

"As always," said Winger, allowing some impatience to show. "Now will you, please, initiate the Resurrect Processing?"

"Cardigan, Jake," said the desk. "His sentence of fifteen years wasn't supposed to be up for another eleven years, was it?"

"It's up today, right now," said the robot. "Therefore, I'd appreciate your acting on my request for his immediate reactivation."

"Of course, Winger (M6)/SCPS-30 PB." The desk made three

low chime sounds. "Resurrection Processing for Prisoner #19,587 has been formally requested and will begin shortly."

Winger didn't bother to correct the desk about his name the second time. "I'll go wait in the Resurrect Wing," he said and rose.

The robot left the room and entered a long, curving, gray corridor. Before he'd covered even half its length a side door came hissing open.

A frail, dark-haired man whose skin was nearly the same shade as the gray walls came rolling into the corridor, riding in a dark metal servochair. "I want to talk to you, Winger," he said. "About why you're taking Jake Cardigan away from here."

Winger watched the chair come rolling quietly toward him. "Dr. Goodhill," he said. "You're looking well."

Goodhill touched a control panel at the side of his chair, causing it to brake to a halt. "Spare me the bullshit," he said in his thin, weary voice. "I'm dying and that's obvious. I won't even be in this hole much longer."

"One more example of the folly of using inferior materials to build with." Tapping his metal chest, the big gleaming robot squatted beside the dying doctor. "How long before you retire?"

"Fairly soon. This began as a sort of retirement—I came up to the Freezer as an Admissions Therapist when I realized I couldn't hold down my job with the Southern California State Police any—"

"I have access to your bio, Doc," cut in Winger, "if that's all you wanted to chat about."

Wheezing slightly, the frail psychiatrist touched the controls again. A jointed metal auxiliary arm snaked up from the side of his chair to dangle a sheet of pale blue paper in front of the crouching robot's face. "Why's Jake being released?" asked Goodhill.

"I happen to be, as you well know, only a functionary," replied

Winger. "I deliver special prisoners up here. I also come to spring certain ones who've been granted an early resurrect."

"Does this mean he's been cleared?"

The robot didn't immediately reply. Instead he shut his chrome eyelids and a faint murmuring hum came spilling out of his skull. "Ah, yes. You and Prisoner #19,587 were once colleagues," he said fourteen seconds later. Letting his eyes snap open, he looked into the therapist's gray face. "In better times you were both dedicated lawmen together—and now look what you've both come to."

"I've always been certain that Jake was framed on those Tek-dealing charges."

"You're really starting to sound like your patients, each and every one of whom swears he's innocent as a lamb."

"He was a good cop—for a hell of a long time. I never believed any of that crap about his being tied in with the Tek runners."

"Remind me to print you up a transcript of his trial sometime." The robot rose up to his full height and frowned down at Goodhill. "After reading over that with an open mind, you won't have any doubts about his guilt."

"I've already read the damn transcript. Once down there, twice since I've been working up here in the Freezer. And it still doesn't convince me," said the doctor. "When I was alerted that you'd come to revive Jake Cardigan, I thought maybe our esteemed SoCal law system had finally gotten its head out of its—"

"That hasn't happened, Doc. To the best of my knowledge his premature release has nothing to do with any new findings having to do with his guilt or innocence." The robot shrugged his wide shoulders. "But, say, since you're so interested in him—why not come along with me? That way you can be right there on the spot when Prisoner #19,587 returns to the world of the living, Doc. He'd certainly like to see a friendly face upon—"

"I know what I look like now," said Dr. Goodhill, anger giving strength to his voice. "I wouldn't want Jake to see me."

The robot nodded. "Then if that's all . . . ?"

"Yeah—thanks for the information."

"I was built to serve." The robot remained, unmoving, waiting until the chair had taken the frail man out of the corridor and away. Then he made his laughing noise and continued on his way.

Light replaced darkness. Very gradually at first, then with an almost explosive brightness.

He felt pain. It throbbed in his head, went shooting through his entire body. Air, rasping and raw, came rushing into his lungs.

Jake Cardigan gave a convulsive jerk, groped out with his left hand. Everything turned cold all around him and he began to shiver.

A chill metal hand slid under his buttocks. The hand held a rough sponge.

"Mess," croaked a metallic voice. "You made a mess."

Jake got his eyes all the way open and the harsh light overhead made him flinch.

"Sorry," he mumbled to the gunmetal robot that was swabbing the white metal table Jake found himself sprawled on. All sorts of wires and tubes were dangling down over him, and Jake had the feeling that most of them had recently been attached to him.

"Mess," croaked the robot again as it finished its cleaning of the table.

"Voiding of whatever may be left in the bowels and bladder is a common resurrection phenomenon, Cardigan," explained someone back out of his range of vision. "No need to be embarrassed at all."

Jake didn't yet have much curiosity to spare, so he didn't even try to look around and identify the speaker. He had several other things to concentrate on. He was having trouble breathing—the process didn't seem to be automatic anymore. He had to force himself to breathe in and out. He continued to experience a great deal of pain, especially in his head and across his chest. There was cold, too. This small metal-walled room where he'd awakened was chill. He couldn't get control of his shivering or make it stop.

The big dark robot took hold of his arm, yanked him up to a sitting position. He sprayed Jake up and down with some harsh-smelling medicinal mist that came squirting out of his right forefinger. "Stand up," he suggested.

"Give me . . . give me a minute." Being pulled abruptly to this new position had made him dizzy. The gray walls were flickering and the floor was swaying.

Jake sat hunched forward, elbows resting on his bare knees, and watched his naked feet for a few seconds.

"Schedule," said the big robot. "Sufficient time's been devoted to this reanimation."

"That's all right," said the other speaker. "I can look after the prisoner now—forgive me, the former prisoner."

Frowning, Jake struggled to remember something. "Yeah, they say you're not supposed to dream in the Freezer," he said, mostly to himself. "Except . . . I'm pretty sure I did have dreams." The gunmetal robot was moving away from him, lumbering by a plastiglass coffin that sat empty on the chill floor. That must be the box Jake had slept in for fifteen years. The robot left the room. "I dreamt about—what? My childhood . . . yeah, my father especially. Police work. Women . . . several of them. But there was one . . . dark-haired young woman. Now who the hell was she?"

Behind him someone made a metallic throat-clearing noise. "If you're completely finished with your reveries, Cardigan, you can get yourself dressed."

Jake got his head to turn. There was a chrome robot, decked out in a fresh white suit, sitting in the small room's only chair. A black chair. Legs crossed, the robot was watching him. "Winger?" he said.

"None other." Nodding his head slightly, the robot got up. "Garments." He stepped closer, holding out a large seethru plyosack.

"That they are," agreed Jake, making no move to take the sack of clothing.

"We have a shuttle to catch," urged the robot, "not to mention considerable paperwork to get through before we can leave. I suggest you commence dressing."

"Okay, sure, I'll give it a try." Jake looked down at the floor. After taking a deep breath, he boosted himself off the metal cot. About a second or so after his bare feet touched the floor he became woozy again. The floor teetered and flipped Jake over. He hit it with both knees, put out a hand to keep from toppling over completely. His stomach made rude noises.

The white-suited robot offered no help. "It will take you perhaps as long as an hour to regain full control of your body again."

Gritting his teeth, Jake pushed with the palms of both hands. He closed his eyes for a few seconds, shoved, succeeded in getting himself upright. He was a man in his late forties, of middle height, with sandy hair. He was close to being handsome, but in a weather-beaten sort of way. Right now he was pale and the various scars and wounds he'd collected stood out on his body. "I'm remembering you now, Winger," he said. "We never much got along when I was a cop."

"Chiefly because you have an unreasoning bias against mechanical beings—from servos to androids," said the robot. "That accounts for it."

"You're also a mean, uncaring son of a bitch," said Jake. "That accounts for it, too."

Winger made his laughing noise. "Exactly. Which is why I'm the one who's here to greet you on awakening and you're the one who's been napping in a prison coffin."

Jake opened the sack of clothes. "So it's fifteen years later, huh?"

"Not exactly, no. Actually it's only been four."

Jake was getting into a pair of shorts. He stopped, balancing on one foot. "Only four—why the hell is that?" he asked the robot. "Did they realize I was innocent after all?"

"I have no hard information as to why you've been granted a Special Parole."

"Special Parole," he said, resuming his dressing. "That means somebody intervened—pulled strings, used influence. You must know who did that, Winger."

"I have no data whatsoever," said Winger. "As soon as you finish, Cardigan, we can go see about checking out."

"Checking out?" Jake laughed. It was the first time he'd done that in a while—well, in four years apparently—and the laugh sounded rusty to him. But it was laughter and basically he felt good about being up and around and able to do it. "Checking out has a pleasant civilized sound. Makes me feel like I've been staying in a hotel and not a prison."

The computer terminal sounded very sympathetic. "On behalf of Warden Niewenhaus," it was saying to Jake, "we wish you well in your imminent return to society. The warden regrets not being here in person, Former Prisoner #19,587, to send you personally back into the world of 2120. Unfortunately some unexpected quake damage to one of his aboveground condos in the Bel Air Sector of Greater Los Angeles requires him to be elsewhere. He has, however, authorized me to pass along his good wishes. Even though you haven't served your full sentence, Warden Niewenhaus is confident you've learned your lesson and will never return here to the Southern California Cryobiotic Penal Institute. Or, for that matter, to any of the fifty-three other prisons and correctional facilities in the State of Southern California . . ."

The chrome Winger leaned in his chair, which was flush next to the one Jake was occupying. "You're not paying close attention to this farewell address," he admonished in a tinny whisper. "This is meant to be uplifting."

Jake had been concentrating on trying to fill out the assorted release forms he'd been handed on entering this gray oval room. He had them all on a metal clipboard that rested on his lap, but the pen kept shaking in his hand. "Having a slight problem writing," he admitted to the robot.

". . . you once were a law-abiding, nay, a law-enforcing citizen of GLA. Therefore, it seems that you ought to be able to return to . . ."

Winger said, "The shakes is a common aftereffect of the reanimation process."

"How long do they last?"

"Not more than an hour usually."

"Usually?"

"Relax, Cardigan. There's nothing at all wrong with you, nothing serious," Winger assured him. "The medics have already determined that."

"I don't recall consulting with any medics recently."

"It was all done when you were being hooked up in the reanimation room. The whole exam was carried out while you still slumbered."

"Very efficient." Jake gave writing another try. This time he could control his hand well enough to scribble a fuzzy approximation of his signature on the various forms where it was required.

". . . any questions that I may answer for you on the brink of your departure, Former Prisoner #19,587?"

Jake looked up at the voxbox of the terminal that sat on a plastand a few feet in front of him. "Yeah, as a matter of fact," he said. "I'd like to know exactly why I'm being turned loose eleven years early?"

There was a silent wait of thirty-one seconds. "We have no information on that," replied the voice of the computer. "The warden suggests that you simply enjoy your newfound freedom and not worry about—"

"Has it got something to do with a review of my case?"

"No."

"Who interceded to get me—"

"We have three more departing prisoners to process," said the terminal, allowing a shade of impatience to sound in its voice. "Permit me to return your belongings to you."

A two-foot-square slot whirred open in the floor near Jake's booted feet and a plasbox popped up into the room.

The box contained Jake's ID packet, his Banx card—a long time expired—a wad of plazpaper money and his lazgun. Jake distributed the stuff in the pockets of his new, and not exactly well-fitting, suit. He saved the weapon for last, holding it up toward Winger. "How come the gun?" he inquired as he tucked it in his waistband.

"Your particular parole allows you to carry weapons."

"That's unusual. It means somebody has had to—"

"Have you finished scrawling your name on all those papers?"

Jake nodded. "Each and every one."

Winger stood, took the forms from Jake's hand. Stooping, he tossed them into the slot that had produced Jake's belongings. "We can take our leave now, unless you have some reason for lingering."

"Nope," Jake assured him, "none at all."

4

When the shuttle was five minutes out of the departure area, Jake took one quick look back at the Freezer. "Sky Academy," he murmured. He stopped looking at the great dark prison colony and looked instead toward Earth.

There were only two other passengers on the flight down to the Greater Los Angeles Spaceport, a large blonde woman of forty and a thin boy of seventeen. They were sitting five rows behind Jake and the robot.

"He's dying," the woman said, starting to cry quietly.

"Cork it, Maw."

"You can tell by looking at him in that pathetic plastiglass box. He's dying, wasting away."

"Jeez, Maw, he looks exactly the fucking same as he did when we visited him at Xmas."

"No, he's getting a lot thinner, Ogden."

"He was always thin, Maw. I ought to know, since the kids at school were always razzing me on account of I had such a skinny fucking father."

"Do you think he knows we visit him?"

"Oh, sure, yeah. Didn't you notice his little skinny mouth breaking out into a big grin when those robot bastards wheeled in his coffin?"

"I'm being serious, Ogden. Fifteen years is such an awful long time to be asleep."

"Maw, sometimes you act like you been asleep your whole entire life yourself."

Winger nudged Jake in the side. "The tragedy of a fifteen-year sentence," he commented quietly.

Jake said, "Now that we're clear of the Freezer—why don't you tell me what's really going on?"

The robot shrugged. "You've been granted a Special Parole. There are no further details."

"But somebody has to have changed his mind. They must realize I wasn't involved in any Tek dealing."

Shaking his gleaming head, Winger replied, "This much I can tell you. There is no one, not a single soul, in the SoCal legal system—that includes judges, cops, attorneys—who still doesn't firmly believe that you are guilty as charged four years ago."

He tapped the gun at his waist. "But someone with influence had to arrange this parole," persisted Jake. "Did my wife have anything to do with it?"

"She's not an especially influential person, is she?"

"She knows some influential people."

"Yes, so my files show. Her one-time employer was Bennett Sands, for example, and he's a very important man in worldwide business circles." The robot steepled his chrome fingers against his chrome nose. "Neither your wife nor Sands had anything to do with your resurrection, Cardigan. In fact, I doubt if Sands would be especially anxious to have you— Ah, but that's none of my business."

Jake eyed him. "What are you hinting at?"

"Nothing," answered the robot. "I must say, by the way, that it's somewhat strange to see you turning to a robot for help. According to your records—and I've studied the lot—you always preferred to work, back in the days when you were allegedly an honest cop, with human officers rather than androids and robots."

"I've worked with plenty of mechs, too. But, sure, I prefer—"

"We consider the term mech an insult."

"So do I," said Jake evenly. "It's always seemed to me that since mechanisms have no real feelings, they can't have hunches. That's why they don't make the best cops—or the best companions."

"Hunches and emotions don't have anything to do with police work," said Winger. "And it seems to me that all your troubles, culminating in your stay up in the Freezer"—he pointed ceilingward with one gleaming thumb—"all those troubles grew out of your emotional problems. First you became dependent on electronic brain stimulation by way of Tek and the Brainbox. Next you got yourself mixed up in the activities of the big-money Tek runners. You sold out your colleagues for dough in order to—"

"No, I didn't," broke in Jake. "I was a tekkie, yeah. I used the stuff and I don't deny that. But I never worked for any of those bastards and I never sabotaged a single police investigation that I was involved with."

"Sounds very convincing," observed the robot. "And it sounded pretty good at your trial, too, when your lawyer put you on the stand. But, alas, the judge, the jury and even the Judicial Review Computer never believed you. Their mutual conclusion was, to put it in layman's terms—horseshit."

Jake laughed, shaking his head. "I guess I've been on ice too long," he said, leaning back in his seat. "Sitting here arguing with a robot."

"You're a lot likelier to get a straight story from me than you are from any of your human friends," the robot told him. He unzipped his jacket and his shirt. "Here now is something I'm required to pass out to all returnees."

The robot's chest whirred and hummed for nearly a half minute. Then a small booklet emerged from the slot in his chrome chest.

Jake asked, "Do you ever run out of paper?"

"This is a brief review of the major changes that have taken place in the world since you left it," Winger said, handing the yellow booklet to him. "We cover politics, entertainment, sports and several other topics."

Accepting it, Jake thrust the booklet in a jacket pocket. "I guess I do have some catching up to do."

"You'll discover that all the important changes aren't in there, for reasons of space," said the robot. "So for some things, Cardigan, you'll simply have to live and learn."

Twilight was spilling rapidly across Greater Los Angeles. Beyond the domes of the spaceport the oncoming darkness was filling in the spaces between the buildings, towers and spires of the various sectors. Windows of a hundred hues were blossoming with light. The flitting skycraft glowed and glittered and the floating billboards started flashing on with multicolored intensity.

Jake came down the disembark ramp from the shuttle slowly. He found he could walk pretty well now, but he didn't want to push his luck.

"This is as far as I'm obliged to escort you." The white-suited robot was walking two paces to the rear of Jake. "You'll hear from me once a month—for the time being at any rate. And, of course, should you have any problems, feel free to contact me by vidphone at any hour."

"I'm not anticipating any problems that you'd be good for." Jake spoke without turning. They'd entered the reception area and he was scanning it.

There were no people around at all. The dozen pale green plaschairs were empty, and in a shadowy corner a dented servobot was mopping the floor very slowly. On the far wall a cluster of adscreens were playing to nobody. Naked girls vacationed at a Brazilian spa on one picscreen, on another a skyball star was extolling a popular brand of marihuana cigarettes, on another a beautiful red-haired woman was holding up a model of a Moon condo.

"I thought," said Jake, stopping in front of a row of empty chairs, "that relatives had to be notified about a release from the Freezer. It used to be the law."

"It still is."

"What about my wife and son? Weren't they—"

"My duties don't include the handling of such details as that."

Jake started walking again. "Do we still live in the same place?"

"Yes, you do."

"There's nothing wrong—with Kate or Dan?"

"Not a thing, far as my records show."

"I was expecting they'd be . . ." He let the sentence die. There was no need to share what he felt with the robot.

Winger made his laughing sound. "Well, welcome home, Cardigan." He patted him on the back with his metal hand, then turned and started walking away. "Try not to do anything that'll get you back in the Freezer."

Jake hesitated, then crossed the threshold and stepped out into the night street. The spaceport door whispered shut behind him and he started walking toward an aircab stand up the block.

He coughed once, twice again. The air felt even fouler than it had four years ago.

"Maybe that's because I've been away," he reminded himself, "and out of the habit of breathing this stuff."

Coughing once more, he increased his pace. He'd decided to head for home without vidphoning his wife. Better just to walk in on her—and Kate probably had a good reason for not meeting him.

Jake stopped next to the aircab at the front of the line of three, a battered orange one. "Can you take me to the Pasadena Sector?"

A roundheaded robot was slouched in the pilot seat. "Huh?" he asked, sitting up, rattling a bit internally and then gazing out at Jake.

Jake leaned closer to the open window. "Pasadena Sector?"

"Sure, sure. Hop in, buddy." The rear door hissed, then came flapping open. "Is there any blood still back there?"

Jake had one foot into the cabin. "Don't see any."

"Sometimes the servos do a lousy job of cleaning up messes like that. I guess it's okay now, so climb aboard."

Sitting on the backseat, Jake asked, "Why was there blood back here?"

"Huh?" The robot cabbie whacked himself on the side of the head with the heel of a coppery fist. "All that shooting this A.M. must've futzed up my hearing. That happens sometimes."

"Shooting?"

"Where to, by the way?"

Jake gave him the address to their underground condo, realizing this was the first time he'd said that in four years. "Did you get involved with the police?"

"No, just minor Tek wars." The robot muttered some instructions to the dash controls. The cab shook, rattled, went rising straight up into the night. "See, there's this guy who turns out to be a Tek-chip pusher riding back there—that was this morning around five A.M. All at once we get forced down. These bastards used a disabler beam on us and there's a big *Futt!* and we drop about five hundred feet and smack the sand. It was, see, over the Malibu Sector. *Futt!* and we drop. Then, I swear, six Japs pile out of an airvan, come charging across the beach with lazguns waving. One of them, a big hefty guy, he's using one of those new needle guns. You know, it shoots *Bap! BAP! BAP!* and fifty or sixty little steel needles dipped in nerve poison come shooting out. Almost all of them hit this rival pusher who's riding in my crate. They just about stitch the poor guy to the seat. Blood starts splashing all over and the poor gink starts going into spasms and then convulsions. Made one hell of a mess. You ever see anything like that?"

"Few times." Jake looked down through the seethru floor of the aircab at the Greater Los Angeles they were flying over.

He noticed that there were the usual fires burning out in the canyons. Passing over the sprawling city where he used to work, Jake became increasingly unsettled by the view. Hundreds of changes had taken place since he'd been put to sleep, some of them major. Another tower had been added to the Southern California State Police complex in the LA Heart Sector and the Military Veterans Hospice in the Old Hollywood Sector, where his father had spent his last months, wasn't down there at all anymore. Another string of bright-lit floating restaurants had been added at the 1500-foot level of pedramps out at the edge of the New Hollywood Sector. There'd apparently been a serious monorail accident within the past hour and two burn-gutted passenger cars were still dangling high in the air near the Beverly Glen transfer. A crew of workmen in hover-packs were working on the tangle with laztorches while a copter-crane came rising up to go to work.

A lot more aboveground housing had been built out over the

Pacific shoreline, too. Jake found the whole experience was like looking at a picture you thought you were familiar with, but that now seemed subtly altered.

Jake shut his eyes, trying to relax. "Kate is sure to know what's going on," he told himself. "About why I was let out early. Sure, more than likely she's had something to do with this."

Jake had married fairly late, when he was getting damn close to thirty-five. He'd come near marrying a couple of times before, but hadn't. With Kate, though, he'd been absolutely sure. And she had told him she was equally certain she loved and wanted him.

"That was true, wasn't it?" Jake asked himself as they flew home across the deepening night. "Sure, Kate always loved me—and she was faithful. Any of my doubts must just be because—"

"I didn't catch what you just said, buddy," apologized the robot cabbie. "Because of my hearing problem, you know."

"Nothing, sorry. Thinking out loud."

"It's one of those days. That's how I been feeling ever since those damn Japs started swarming all over us."

Toward the last few months there, just before Jake was arrested, he'd started wondering about Kate. Sometimes it was tough to turn off being a cop. You tend to see clues and evidence everywhere.

They had one child, a son named Dan. Jake of course had intended to bring up Dan a good deal differently from the way he'd been raised. With more closeness and a lot more affection shown. But that hadn't exactly worked out. The police life has a way of taking your time and—well, it just never worked out as well as he'd hoped. He and Dan were close, though, Jake had made sure of that. He'd seen to it they spent time together. Not as much as he wished, but some. Dan grew into a good kid, bright and honest.

". . . place, isn't it, buddy?"

Straightening up, Jake looked around him.

The aircab was settling down to a landing in the small illuminated sylvan park area that masked the entrance to the underground building where he lived with his wife and eleven-year-old— No, wait—Dan would be fifteen now.

"Yes, this is it. Thanks." He paid the fare from the cash they'd returned to him up in the Freezer. "Hope you don't have any further trouble."

"You and me both, buddy." The aircab climbed up and went chugging away, passing over dozens of similar small parks.

The plaslites planted in the faketurf of Jake's park made the leaves of the trees—all of which were real—glow bright green. The mechanical birds were still twittering the same song they'd sung four years ago.

"At least one thing hasn't changed while I was away." Jake started for the stairway that led down to the elevator room.

A very handsome android butler, dressed in gray livery, was walking a platinum-haired poodle along a hedge-lined path. He looked human, except for his eyes, which, in obvious need of repair, were blinking much too rapidly. "Evening, gov," he said in a very realistic voice.

"Good evening." At the entry door Jake pressed the palm of his right hand to the IDscan. Six seconds went by and then the tiny voxbox mounted just below the scanner barked, "Cardigan—22C—enter."

The metal door quivered and slid aside.

Jake crossed into the elevator area. The door of the cage on the far right in the row of three opened and he stepped in. "Twenty-two," he requested.

The elevator recognized him. "Good evening, Mr. Cardigan," it said amiably from its overhead voxbox. "I trust you had a nice day."

"Matter of fact," answered Jake, grinning, "today has been quite a bit better than most of them lately."

"Glad to hear that."

The cage dropped swiftly down to the twenty-second level of the underground condo complex. It opened its door, cautioning, "Watch your step, Mr. Cardigan. Good evening."

As Jake neared his door, he heard odd noises and scurrying sounds from inside. Drawing his lazgun, he opened the door and dived inside.

5

A squat silvery servomech was vacuuming the rug, a taller round one with a half dozen long spidery arms was dusting the cassette shelves.

There was no one in the living room.

Jake entered, scanning the place and wondering why the servos had picked this particular time to tidy up. "Kate?" he said tentatively, then repeated it more loudly. "Kate?"

Gun still in his hand, Jake shut the door behind him and crossed the carpet. Things looked just about the same as they had four years ago, except the apartment computer terminal sat on a new stand. The carpeting in the hall was new, too, and a shimmering shade of blue.

"Kate? It's me—Jake." He moved slowly along the hallway.

No response.

Behind him in the living room the servomechs finished up their chores, put themselves away in their wall compartments.

The master bedroom hadn't changed much either. The wide circular bed was neatly made. New spread, some glittery kind of cloth Jake wasn't familiar with. "Probably one of those new synthetics from the Moon Colony mills," he decided.

He touched the palm of his hand to a yellow-tinted patch of wall across from the bed. The IDpanel gave a ping of recognition and a portion of the wall slid aside. The interior light squares turned on. All of Jake's clothes—the civilian stuff anyway, since his uniforms had been turned in after his conviction—were hanging there on two long lucite rods.

"But Kate's things are gone." Unless she was storing her wardrobe someplace else these days. "That's possible, I guess. In four years people can change their habits."

But down in his son's room there was nothing. No bed, no clothes, no clutter. A blank, white-walled room, the carpeting smelling faintly of self-cleaning chemicals.

"Mr. Cardigan, Mr. Cardigan." It was the voice of the condo computer calling him from the living room.

"Yes, what?"

"Mr. Cardigan, I have an important message from your wife—Mrs. Kathleen McRobb Cardigan."

"That wife, huh?" He went striding down the hall. "Glad you finally remembered." Jake perched on a sofa arm, eyeing the small black terminal.

"Mrs. Kathleen McRobb Cardigan regrets to inform you that she has divorced you, Mr. Jonathan Cardigan, Jr.," said the terminal. It sounded like it had the same voice as the terminal who'd given him the farewell pep talk up in the Freezer. "That occurred exactly two years and sixteen days ago in the Civil Court of the State of Southern California, Pasadena Sector Annex, Robojudge XX-30F-227 presiding. Divorce granted under the Absent Criminal Act of 2107."

Jake had started to stand, but he sat back down. He noticed the gun in his hand, leaned and placed it carefully on the plastiglass coffee table. "Two years ago—why didn't anybody tell me?"

"It is not possible to convey information of any kind to a comatose prisoner incarcerated in the—"

"Why didn't somebody tell me today? That silver-plated Winger, for instance."

"That I do not know," replied the voxbox. "Your former wife

further wishes you to be informed that she no longer resides in the State of Southern California or in the United States of America as a whole. She and your former son, Daniel Jonathan Cardigan, have resettled in Mexico and—"

"Former son?"

"—are both in the best of health. They do not, neither of them, at this point in time wish to communicate directly with you. At some later date, should their feelings about the suitability of contact with you change to any degree, you shall be notified by an authorized legal representative of the former Mrs. Cardigan."

"That's fine, great."

"This condo was transferred entirely to your name at the time of the divorce decree and is now yours to do with as you wish, Mr. Cardigan. Half of your joint savings remain in the Banx system, and once you have reactivated your Banx card, under the terms set forth in the Resurrected Criminals, Returned Lunatics and Pardoned Rapists Act of 2097, you will have access to $41,684.87. That amount includes interest accumulated over four years plus half the amount realized from the sale of your aircar as well as what was realized from your adjusted Police Employee Retirement Plan. This message was set to be delivered to you upon your return to—"

"You said four years," cut in Jake, "meaning Kate must've known I was coming out today. How'd she find out?"

"I do not know. This latest version of the message from Mrs. Cardigan was fed into our system at four P.M. today, SoCal time."

"From where?"

"The place of origin is logged in simply as 'Somewhere in Mexico.' "

"Zero in on that, if you can, and get me more details."

After a few seconds the computer told him, "I am unable to obtain any further information."

"You don't have an address or vidphone number for my wife—excuse it, former wife?"

"Such information is unavailable at this time. Can I provide you any further service or—"

"The phone." Jake was looking around the living room. "Where's it stored these days?"

"The same place. I will activate it."

A panel in the far wall slid silently open, revealing the phone alcove. It was furnished with a padded metal chair, a stand and a vidphone.

"Pink?" Jake crossed to it.

"The former Mrs. Cardigan switched from black phone to pink phone three years ago."

Shrugging one shoulder, Jake stepped into the alcove and seated himself facing the small rectangular screen.

The heavyset black woman shook her head again. "Wish I could, Jake," she said apologetically.

Frowning at the image on the phonescreen, he said, "Sure, I understand, Onita."

"When you were with the SCSP it was different," the middle-aged woman explained. "But now—well, now your status ain't exactly fragrant anymore. Besides which, Pacific Videocom is a lot tougher than it was back in your law and order days about giving out restricted numbers."

"I'll get Kate's number some other way, thanks."

She smiled. "Hey, anyway, I'm glad you're out, Jake. You figuring to stay out?"

"That's one of my major goals in life," he assured her, grinning and killing the call. Jake sank back in the stiff chair for a few seconds, massaging the bridge of his nose. "Not going to be as easy as I thought."

"Beg pardon?" said the condo computer terminal.

"Wasn't talking to you."

"Perhaps I might summon a house medic for you?"

"No need, nope." He straightened, punched out another number.

A large dented robot, his bare metal torso scribbled with an assortment of lewd graffiti in various basic colors, appeared on the screen. "Varney the Vampire's Bar & Grill, Santa Monica Sector. Yeah, what?"

"I want to contact Newsboy O'Hearn."

"Where you been, asshole?"

"Away."

"Well, so is O'Hearn. The asshole vanished without a frigging trace three years ago," said the bartender robot. "Theory at the time was he maybe got himself teleported to an especially faraway place by some competitor or a disgruntled hoodlum. Anything else?"

"How about Cyborg Slim?"

"You could maybe try Mom's Café down in the Manhattan Beach Sector. Say, you're Cardigan, aren't you?"

"I am."

"Some go in, some come out. That's the way of the frigging world when you come to think of it. See you." He broke the connection.

After sighing slightly, Jake tried another number.

Mom herself, a frail woman of fifty, answered. "Cardigan! Welcome back to the living," she said. "You look great, just the same—but that's to be expected, seeing as you been in suspended animation. Myself, I'm not looking so good."

"I won't lie to you, Mom, you're not. What's wrong?"

"I'm not sure, but about two years ago I took a strong and violent dislike to the kind of food I serve in this joint and I don't seem to be able to eat much any longer."

"Try dining out."

"Naw, I can't do that, Jake. I'm much too busy cooking here to have time to go out anywhere."

"I'm looking for Cyborg Slim."

"He's not in his old line of work any longer," Mom said. "Cops picked Slim up for info siphoning about six months back. He got sentenced to twenty-five years of amnesia. They did that to him up at the state rehab in the Oxnard Sector and now the poor bastard doesn't remember a damn thing about his former trade—and Slim was one of the best computer tappers in the business. He's driving a skytruck for a hydroponic tomato ranch in the San Diego Sector and has this half-assed smile on his face all the time."

"Maybe I can use Suicide Smith."

"Oh, you haven't heard about him either, have you? Suicide committed suicide last Xmas," Mom told him. "Here we always thought the guy was kidding about wanting to do himself in. I mean, you wouldn't nickname a guy Suicide if you knew he was really going to do it someday. Well, he did it."

"That's too bad," said Jake. "I need a phone number that may be fairly well protected. Anybody else you can suggest, Mom?"

"Wiz Robinson's still around, Jake."

Jake considered that. "I don't know, he's not as reliable as—"

"True, but on the other hand Wiz is above the ground and his brains haven't been frazzled."

"There is that about him. Okay, where can I find him?"

"Let me do that for you," she volunteered. "You at home?"

"Same place." He gave her his number. "I'd like to get the number soon as I can."

"I'll track Wiz down and have him contact you," she promised. "Try to relax and don't get excited. That's the secret of a successful life."

"I've been doing more than my share of relaxing lately." He hung up.

The vidphone screen remained blank. "You're looking good, Jake, looking very good all things considered."

"Wish I could say the same for you, Wiz. Why the blackout?"

"Reasons, I got my reasons," came the whispering voice of the tapper. "Let us simply say, Jake, that Wiz Robinson is lying low."

"Okay by me. Now listen, Wiz, what I need is—"

"Your opinion of my abilities hasn't been very high, not high at all. Tonight, however, it's going to change. I have anticipated, making some clever deductions from the hints that Mom dropped, your request and gone to work."

"What are you telling me, Wiz—that you have the vidphone number I want?"

"Exactly, Jake, that's exactly what I am telling you," the blank screen informed him. "You want the phone number of your erstwhile missus—isn't that so?"

"Yeah, I do. Have you got it?"

"Of course I do, of course. The little lady—quite a looker from all accounts—is residing in Mexico, across the border in the state of Quintana Roo. Do you need the exact spelling of this unusual and musical name?"

"No, I've been there."

"Spent your youth across the border, yes, it comes back to me now," continued Wiz. "The little lady—who continues to call herself Kathleen Cardigan, by the way, if you want to take that as a sign of anything, although most of my exes still go around dubbed Mrs. Robinson and they, all and sundry, hate me like vile poison. The little lady's present phone number and address are as follows." He provided Jake with a Mexican vidphone number and the address of the small villa where Kate was living.

"I appreciate this, Wiz."

"Think nothing of it, Jake. It's merely another example of the sort of first-class service I provide my customers, even customers who have been going around saying I'm a second-rater."

"What about my son—is he living there, too?"

"The lad is away at school, but I don't as yet have full details. Do you want that stuff, too?"

"Want all the information I can get on them," Jake told the blank screen. "Now, how much do I owe you, Wiz?"

"Nothing, not a peso," replied the informant. "This has been a free sample, Jake, a demo of my exceptional gifts in the area of unauthorized-information retrieval. Should you want all I can gather on the kid, it'll cost you two hundred dollars."

Jake said, "Okay, it's a deal."

"Might there be, Jake, anything else I could unearth for you?"

"I can use anything on why I was paroled from the Freezer."

"Noted, noted and jotted down in my infallible memory," said Wiz. "I bid you now a fond good evening."

"Good night, Wiz, and thanks."

Jake clicked off the phone. He pushed back in the chair and stood.

He slowly circled the living room, first with his hands in his pockets and then with them behind his back. "Go ahead and call her," he urged himself after five minutes of pacing.

Jake took a deep breath, returned to the alcove. He punched out the number Wiz had given him.

The zigzag rainbow patterns indicating an out-of-the-country call flashed briefly across the phonescreen. Then a face appeared. It was the nearly blank metallic face of an inexpensive answering 'bot—one eye and a voxbox. "Cardigan residence," the robot said.

"Kate Cardigan, please." Maybe the fact that she was still using the name was a good sign. Meaning she still felt a link with him.

"Identify yourself, if you will."

"I'm Jake Cardigan."

The single white eye glowed, briefly, green. "Please stand by, Mr. Cardigan."

The robot faded, its image replaced by blackness. Thirty seconds went by.

"Kate," Jake said when she appeared. "Listen, I—"

"Hi, Jake. I figured you'd be able to track me down eventually and so I'm making this tape for when you call," his wife—make that former wife—was saying.

He leaned forward, frowning, watching the picture on the phonescreen. Kate had changed in four years. She was thinner for one thing, at least ten pounds lighter. Her auburn hair was cut differently, much shorter, and she appeared to be—what? Tired. Uneasy. Yeah, a little of both. She also looked as though she might be recuperating from something, a virus maybe.

"Have you been sick?" he asked, before remembering he was trying to question a recording.

". . . want you to know I'm fine," Kate was saying.

She sat in a wingback white rattan chair out in a walled redstone and adobe patio. There was sunlight and a lot of bright foliage and flowers surrounding her. The tape had apparently been made this afternoon.

"Dan is doing very well. He was accepted by a very fine prep school down here and he's getting good grades in his major subjects."

"What are they?" Jake didn't even know what his son was studying, what he wanted to be. Dan had always said he was going to be a cop. But that was four years ago, when he was eleven, and before Jake had been sent up to the Freezer.

". . . best that right now we don't see you. We both, as you must know, wish you only the best in life, Jake. And perhaps sometime in the future we'll all be able to get together." Kate paused, glancing down at her folded hands. "I'm not saying this to hurt you—please understand that—but Danny was terribly upset by what happened. He'd admired you so much and then—well, it took a long time for him to get over that, to accept the fact his father was in prison. Seeing you just now, I'm afraid, would only—"

"I was innocent!" shouted Jake at the screen. "You know that, Kate—so does Dan."

". . . if you'd remained up in the Freezer for the full fifteen years, it might be different. But four years, Jake, simply hasn't been long enough for Danny to adjust to all that's happened."

"If I stayed the whole sentence, he'd be twenty-six when I got loose. Probably married and with kids of his own and only a vague idea of who the hell I was."

". . . please keep in mind that I have no bad feelings toward you. I did, after all, love you once. I'm sure that now you're free you'll be able to build some sort of very satisfying life for yourself. But that life can't have anything to do with Dan and myself. You're a good man, Jake—good luck."

She was gone. The screen was blank.

Angry, he punched out her number again. "I've got to talk to her directly."

A different robot appeared. A polished chrome one with a vaguely humanoid face. "Good evening, I'm WC/1587, your Pacific Vidphone operator," it said. "How may I be of service?"

"I'm trying to reach this number."

"That particular phone is no longer in service, sir."

"I was just talking to it."

The gleaming robot replied, "That's possible, but it is presently out of service. In fact, vidphone communication will not be resumed on that number for the immediate future."

"Is there an alternate number?"

"None whatsoever, sir," answered the robot operator. "We can, however, send you a faxgram notification if and when the number does go back into service. Would you care to have us do that?"

"You might as well."

"The standard charge for faxgram notification is twenty-five dollars, Mr. Cardigan. That will automatically be billed to your account."

Nodding and ending the call, he left the alcove.

Jake paced again. "Okay, it sounds like the marriage is definitely over and done," he said. "The best thing for me to—"

"Is there something I can do for you, sir?" asked the computer terminal.

"Yep, you can quit asking me if there's something you can do."

"Keep in mind that it's my duty to—"

"Just shut up for now."

Jake went over and sat on the sofa. He got up to pace. He sat in an armchair. He got up to pace.

"What you're going to have to do is leave her alone," he told himself finally. "At least for a while. Eventually you'll have to work out something so that you can see Dan—and since when did she call him Danny?"

He wandered down the hall and into the bedroom. Kneeling, he shouldered the wide round bed aside. There was the same small worn patch in the carpeting.

"No, you're through with this damn stuff. Even if it is still there."

He got up, sat on the edge of the bed.

"But who would it hurt?"

It would hurt Jake. And he'd given his word to himself that he wasn't going to use the stuff anymore.

"Hell, it's probably not even there. Kate must've tossed it all out years ago."

Except the little hidden compartment wouldn't open for anyone but him.

"Even so, some of the SCSP investigators must've long since found it and confiscated it."

If they had, how come it hadn't shown up as evidence at his trial? They'd showed plenty of other evidence pointing to his involvement with Tek.

"Okay, all right. Let's find out."

Back on his knees, he pressed his palm flat on the worn spot. The recognition ping sounded and the expertly concealed panel in the rug popped up open to reveal a small compartment hidden in the bedroom floor.

And everything was there. He saw his spare Brainbox, the plastiglass vial that still held three good usable Tek chips and the electrodes to attach to his head.

Remaining in the kneeling position, Jake stared down into the hole.

7

Jake had shoved the bed back into place and was sitting atop it, boots off and feet up, leaning back against the wall. Arranged alongside him was his Tek gear, which he hadn't used in several weeks—

"It's been four years," he reminded himself.

Intellectually he knew he'd been up in the Freezer all that time, but he still didn't feel as though he'd been away at all. He'd said goodbye to Kate at the spaceport that morning—Dan had been left at home—and boarded the prisonbound shuttle. They'd put him to sleep about two hours after he got up there, pausing only for a quick physical and a quick psychiatric evaluation. Then he was awakened and told it was four years later.

And, yeah, it really was April 3, 2120. He'd confirmed that from the vidnews a little while ago.

He scowled. "There was something I dreamed about, something important." He tried again to remember, but couldn't retrieve it.

Jake picked up his Brainbox. It was black and silver, fitting comfortably in his hand, and was shaped something like an old-fashioned pocket calculator. The headset, which Jake picked up next, consisted of a ring of flexible alloy and three contact-electrodes. You just plugged the headset cord into the side of the box. Jake did that now, then swung the trio of electrodes back and forth a few times in his left hand.

"What difference would it really make?"

There was no one here, and the apartment wasn't bugged. He'd determined that before taking the gear out of its hole. He had enough chips, three of them, for at least three hours on the box.

"I'll only do one, though."

One would be enough. He'd do an hour of Tek and then quit. Quit for good probably. That would prove he could handle the stuff and wasn't dependent on it anymore.

"I think I can state, without fear of contradiction, that this has been one hell of an exceptional day."

If you only used Tek once in a while—at times like now, when the stress level started rising—then you weren't actually hooked at all.

"Bullshit." He dropped the gear to the bed. "You can't let yourself start again at all."

He was breathing more rapidly now, starting to sweat.

A single Tek chip wasn't going to do him any harm.

"Besides, you've only got three in all. Once those are used up, that'll be it. You sure as hell aren't going to buy any Tek after that."

Picking up the small plastiglass vial between thumb and forefinger, Jake held it up and gave it a gentle shake.

"Just three."

He opened the vial, extracted a chip, shut it and dropped it onto the bed.

The silicon chip was roughly the size of an average cockroach and had two rows of five tiny spikes along its underbelly. You inserted it into the chip-socket on the top side of the Brainbox. That powered the box, providing you with the opportunity for any sort of fantasy you desired.

Casually Jake picked up the Brainbox. He clicked the chip into place and rested the box on his lap.

"Everything should still fit." He slipped the headset on, adjusting it so the electrodes touched the three spots on his head that would allow for maximum brain stimulation.

Looking down at the Brainbox, he let his right hand hover over it. There was a key pad just below the socket. You ordered your specific fantasy that way.

A fairly simple gadget really. Most law officials agreed that the first Tek chips had surfaced about thirty years ago, but they didn't agree on who invented the Brainbox system. The consensus was that the earliest ones had showed up near the Kyoto Institute of Technology in Japan. But several of the anti-Tek agents Jake had known insisted that Tek and the box were a product—a bootleg product, of course—of a military research lab that had existed for a time on the outskirts of Sweetwater, Texas.

Didn't really matter. The stuff worked.

Suddenly, rapidly, Jake pushed the activate switch. Next he tapped out a specific brainstim fantasy on the key pad.

Just after he did that someone called him from the living room. "Jake—are you here?"

He snatched the headset off, dumped the whole kit on the bed, dropped a pillow over it and jumped up. He tugged on his boots and went running down the hall. "Kate, is that you?"

"Well, of course." She was standing in the center of their living room, wearing the same pale green fakesilk dress she'd had on in the vidtape. She looked fine now, though, not weary or ill.

"After I got your message, I didn't expect to see you again for a while." He stood smiling at her.

"I know, and I'm really sorry about that." Very hesitantly his wife moved closer and put her arms around him. "That was all just a mistake. So I decided I'd better fly back home. I was really hoping I'd get here before you'd seen the damn tape."

Jake didn't speak, just held on to her, tight, and then kissed her. Finally he said, "Then you don't want to stay divorced?"

Pushing gently back from him, she shook her head. "No, the divorce was a mistake, too," Kate admitted. "You know how lawyers can be. After you'd been away nearly two years—well, one of them convinced me there was no chance at all you'd come back before the fifteen years was up. I really had done everything I could think of to try to get you a parole, but nothing worked. And fifteen years seemed like such a long time." Her head lowered and she started, very quietly, to cry. "I gave up on you, Jake, and I'm sorry."

"It's okay, Kate, it's okay." He took hold of his wife again.

"The important thing is—I've decided I don't want to go through with it, don't want to be away from you any longer."

"Yeah, that's what matters."

"You haven't said anything to Dan."

"Dan? I didn't even notice that he—"

"Hi, Dad. Welcome home." There was a lean young man, hair lighter than Jake's, standing just behind Kate. He was taller than Jake, by about a good inch.

"Dan! My God, you're—Hell, you're just about grown."

"Four years'll do that, Dad." He held out something toward his father. "Here's a present for you, sort of a welcome-home gift."

Jake narrowed his eyes, but he still couldn't quite make out what it was his son was offering him. He couldn't seem to get it in focus. "What is it, kid?"

"I made it for you in one of my classes at school," explained Dan. "I really hope you like it."

"What class was that?"

"Metalcraft."

"Oh, sure, metalcraft." He could see it more clearly now. It was a small bronze statue of a rearing stallion. "It's terrific, Dan."

"We have a very gifted son." Kate put one arm around Jake's waist and one around Dan's. "Now that we're all back together again we can start—what's the matter, Jake?"

"Dan's hair. It looks darker now than when I first—"

"It's been a lot darker than yours for nearly four years now."

"Do you really like the matador, Dad?"

"Matador?"

Dan laughed, pointing at the statue his father held in his left hand. "My gift. I go, you know, to the bullfights a lot since we moved across the border. Mom thinks they're brutal but I like them. That's why I made the statue of a matador for you."

"It's great. Very nicely done." Reaching over, Jake set the small statue on the coffee table. "How about your luggage—where did you leave it?"

"It's all here, Dad. Didn't you notice?"

Two large plastileather trunks and six assorted suitcases—including the tan one Kate had taken along on their honeymoon—were piled on the carpet near the door.

"Didn't see them before." Jake shook his head, laughing. "Too many distractions, I guess."

Kate asked, "Are you two ready for dinner?"

"We can go out someplace," suggested Jake.

"No, no—it's cooked already," said his wife. "I phoned the computer from the airport as soon as we arrived and told it what to prepare. I know you like Mexican food, Jake, so that's what I ordered up."

"Don't both of you get enough of that every day?"

"This is your party, Jake."

He picked up his fork. "It looks fine, my compliments to the computer."

Smiling, Kate reached across the kitchen table to touch her husband's hand. "I'm really glad we're together again," she said. "You don't know how much I've missed you."

"I've missed you, too, Dad."

Jake frowned at him. "I can't get over your hair," he said. "I thought it was much darker."

"Sometimes it is, Dad. But, you know, you haven't seen me for a long time and you can't be expected to know exactly what shade it is now."

"That makes sense, sure." Jake refilled his wineglass, held it up. "Here's to our family."

"Guess what I'm feeling at this moment in time, *amigo?*" asked the compact, dark, curly-haired man who was sitting patiently on the far end of the bed and watching Jake. "I'll supply the answer, since you look like your brains—what few you possess—are still addled." He stood up. "I feel like a schmuck, Jake. Yes, indeed, because I've been busting my ass for months telling people you were a guy who could be trusted and that you really weren't a tekkie at all."

Removing the headset, Jake said, "You're a little late for the homecoming party, Gomez."

As he sat on the living room sofa Jake asked, "How'd you get in?"

Sid Gomez settled into an armchair. "We used to be partners, remember?" He held up his right hand, palm outward. "I'm one of the happy few your condo lets in."

"I'm not really back on Tek," he said. "But this was my first day home and the way things . . . Never mind, you've already heard all the excuses."

Gomez was about ten years younger than Jake, and his tight-curling black hair seemed to have a life of its own, jiggling now as he gave a disappointed shake of his head. "Lately my current wife has taken to alluding to me as an idealistic putz," he said. "And that is chiefly because I've been harboring the halfwit notion that you're savable. But, Jesus, before you're even thawed out from your little siesta in the Freezer, you start zapping your brains with that—"

"Are you the one who got me paroled?"

After watching his friend for a few seconds Gomez replied, "I was instrumental in getting you out."

"Thanks then, even if you do think I'm an asshole."

"You're still about two or three grades from qualifying as an asshole," said his ex-partner. "But a couple more sessions with the Brainbox and—"

"How come you didn't contact me earlier?"

"I wanted to give you a little time to adjust to civilian life."

Jake smiled faintly. "And you wanted to test me, see if I was still hooked," he said. "Doesn't look like I passed the test."

"This wasn't the final exam, *amigo.*"

"You're still optimistic. Don't see how you can be after all your years with the Southern California State Police."

"I'm not a cop anymore, Jake."

"You're not? Then my getting out really doesn't have anything to do with SCSP changing their mind about me and pressuring the Parole Authority?"

Gomez chuckled. "Nope, narrow-minded bastards that they are, they still think you sometimes clamp electrodes on your *cabeza* and have brainstim wet dreams," he said. "You and me, of course, know how wrong they are."

"Goddamn it, Gomez, you know I use the stuff sometimes," he said, his voice rising. "You knew that before I ever got picked up. But you also know I never sold Tek or worked for the GLA dealers. And I sure as hell didn't sabotage the investigation of that Laguna Sector connection. I was trying to bust them."

"That much we agree on." Gomez scratched his head. "For a while there, Jake, while I was still a minion of the law, I kept digging into your case—on my own time."

"Is that why you're not with SCSP anymore—did they dump you for trying to help me?"

"Actually, no. It's more complicated than that," said Gomez. "I thought I was getting close, even had a guy ready to confide in me. Then he suddenly went on to glory, helped along by a blast from a lazrifle."

"Who was this guy?"

"One of our fellow officers—Brian Jessup."

"Jessup." Jake stood and began to pace. "That's funny."

"Share the humor of it with me, *amigo.*"

"Funny as in odd." Jake halted, shrugged. "No, it's only that I've been brooding about Kate and—well, Brian Jessup was interested in her. Few times at parties he paid a little more attention to her than I thought was necessary. She didn't return his interest—far as I know—and I was probably just being your typical old coot with a wife ten years younger than he is."

Gomez was studying his booted feet. "We can talk about your wife at some future get-together," he said. "Right now, though—"

"Is there something about Kate I ought to know?"

"*Nada,* nothing, not a damn thing. Just sit yourself down and attend to what I'm saying."

Frowning, Jake returned to the sofa. "What did Jessup have to say?"

"Whatever the lad knew, he took to the grave with him—or rather the urn, since his wife had him microwave-cremated," explained Gomez. "But he'd been hinting he knew something that might just help prove you'd been set up. Jessup indicated he'd be willing to confide for a suitable financial consideration. Two days before we were going to chat, a mall sniper down in the Apple Valley Sector did him in, along with four shoppers and a show dog."

"Coincidence?"

"It does seem a mite extravagant way of getting rid of the gent, killing four others and a dog worth more than the whole lot of them just to cover the shutting up of Jessup."

"Tek runners aren't noted for being sentimental."

"That is true," admitted his friend. "At any rate, *amigo,* that was about the time I came to the conclusion that a cop's life was no longer for me. With my sterling record, plus my innate and undeniable Latino charm, I had no trouble whatsoever landing a position with the respected Cosmos Detective Agency right here in GLA."

Jake grinned at him. "You mean you're a private eye now?"

"I have been for the past year. Later in the evening I may even show you my badge."

"As I recall, Cosmos is a pretty good outfit."

"Walt Bascom runs it and he's—if you bend your definitions some—honest and reliable," said Gomez. "The pay is much better than a cop's and there are considerably more fringe benefits."

"Was Cosmos involved in getting me out?"

"It took me a long time, Jake, to realize that if I wanted justice for you, I'd have to get it the way most people do," he answered. "By using money and influence. I don't have quite sufficient of either, but Bascom and the Cosmos outfit do. And that's how your Special Parole got arranged."

Jake said, "Does Bascom do favors like that for all his employees—or just for the ones with Latino charm?"

Gomez consulted his feet again. "Actually, Jake, I had to promise the detective agency a favor in return."

"A favor that you do—or one that we both have to work on?"

"Both of us, as a team. And—trust me, *amigo*—it's damn lucky for us that this particular case came up just when it did. Otherwise you might still be languishing in the Freezer."

Jake leaned forward, resting his palms on his knees. "Okay, give me the details on this favor, Gomez."

"First off—you don't, do you, have any major or massive objections to working for Cosmos as an operative yourself?"

Jake shook his head. "Nope."

"Even if you had to, say, travel across the border—into the Borderland and Mexico itself?"

"Nope."

"Even if you might have to enter a war zone that is at present controlled by hot-blooded and wild-eyed rebels?"

"That wouldn't bother me, no."

Gomez nodded, his hair swaying some. "*Bueno.* That's gratifying," he said. "Oh, and one other item. I assume you'd have no serious objection to dealing directly with a former ladyfriend of yours? She is, according to all reports, still *muy bonita* and—"

"Whoa, now." Jake got to his feet. "You're talking about Warbride, aren't you?"

"Well, yes," admitted his friend. "That quaintly nicknamed lady revolutionary is who I am alluding to."

"Why's the Cosmos Detective Agency interested in a small-time guerrilla leader who does a little smuggling on the side?"

"Things have changed considerably down there whilst you've been away. Warbride has upped her status a good deal," Gomez told him. "She now heads a substantial rebel army, and only last month they took over control of the whole blooming state of Chihuahua."

"And this case—it involves Chihuahua?"

"Yep, it does."

"C'mon, Gomez, Cosmos must have ops on staff who know their way around that part of Mexico."

"We had several who thought they did." Gomez shook his head and his hair seemed to bounce. "Three of our operatives thus far have ventured south of the border. None has gotten around to reporting back or even to leaving a clue as to present whereabouts. Bascom now believes, thanks in good measure to my powers of persuasion, that since you and Warbride were once close buddies, you are the man who can get safely into—"

"We weren't friends. We just slept together," Jake said. "That woman is mean-minded, foul-tempered—"

"Let me, Jake, hasten to explain to you that my boss is not exactly as enthusiastic about you as I am. Were you to turn this little chore down, he might well regret he used his considerable influence to get you out of the icebox."

Jake pointed a thumb at the ceiling. "Meaning I might end up back at the Freezer if I don't take this job?"

"It's, *amigo,* a possibility worth mentioning."

Sitting, Jake said, "I tell you, Gomez, the way I'm feeling just now—maybe I wouldn't mind going back up there."

"You're merely suffering from post-Tek depression. That'll pass."

"I'd like to think about it." Jake leaned back. "About whether I want to work for Cosmos or not. But you might as well give me the rest of the details on this case."

Brightening, Gomez extracted three triop photos from an inner pocket of his orange sport jacket. "Here are some visuals for you to contemplate, the two central figures in this business." He handed the pictures across. "Two shots of Dr. Leon Kittridge, age fifty-six. One of his daughter Beth Kittridge, age twenty-six. She's somewhat pretty, huh? Too slim for my taste and I favor blondes, since they're usually more capable of inflicting the sort of nastiness I require seemingly in my dealings with members of the . . . Jake, what's wrong?"

Jake was studying one of the photos, a disturbed expression on his face. The young woman in the three-dimensional photo was dark-haired, slim and pretty. She wore a simple suit-dress and was standing on a sunbright stretch of afternoon beach, smiling in a quiet way. "Nothing really, I guess," he said slowly. "Beth Kittridge looks familiar and—I had the impression I'd seen her recently." He turned his attention again to the two pictures of Dr. Kittridge, a lean, tanned man with short-cropped graying hair. "Obviously I couldn't have seen Beth Kittridge lately, her or anyone else."

"You could have seen both of them before you went away," suggested Gomez. "Kittridge is a well-known electronics expert, worked in industry and taught at universities around here. What you call a prominent member of the scientific community. His daughter is something of an electronics wizard, too, and she's been helping the old boy in his researches of late."

Jake said, "Hey, fifty-six isn't that old. I'm little more than a half dozen years from there myself, Gomez."

"And when you arrive there, I'll call you 'old boy,' too," he said. "Speaking the truth is one of my specialties."

Jake looked again at Beth. "How do the Kittridges tie in with this assignment?"

"They *are* the assignment, *amigo,*" he replied. "Don't, by the way, get too interested in the young lady. It may well turn out that both she and her pop are dead and gone."

Jake dropped all three photos to the table. "Were they killed down in Mexico?"

"That's one of the questions we're going to have to answer," said Gomez. "It seems Dr. Kittridge and his daughter were traveling in Mexico last week in their skycruiser. While they were flying over a Great Forest area the ship maybe crashed. This particular *Selva Grande* now happens to be deep in the territory your pal Warbride and her troops control. All that's come out thus far is a highly suspect report made by some louts who claim to be the local law. They say the ship was apparently wrecked and that both the doctor and Beth are probably dead."

"That's all pretty damn vague."

"Yeah, exactly. One of the big insurance outfits—Moonbase-Hartford actually—that retains Cosmos issued a large life-policy on both the doctor and his daughter. So they want definite proof as to whether either or both of them is dead—or should that be 'are' dead? Either way, that's basically what the job is. We've got to get down there, find out the fate of the Kittridges and live to file a report. Be nice if along the way we also found out what happened to our own ops whom we've lost touch with."

"That forest is part of the worldwide project to control the greenhouse effect," said Jake. "Don't the United Nations forces have ranger stations in the—"

"Nobody can get any word out of that particular *selva.* There are supposed to be two ranger stations devoted to the policing of that million acres of giant trees. But they're simply not reporting in any longer and can't be reached by any traditional means of communication."

Picking up the photos, Jake shuffled them and then brought Beth's to the top. "Be a shame if she's dead," he said.

"Both of them could be dead, both could be alive. Cosmos has to find out which it is." He sat quietly for a few seconds. "Bascom wants to see you *mañana,* by early afternoon at the latest. We're obliged to move fast on this—and the Moonbase-Hartford folks are growing, with some justification, a bit impatient."

"You and I will be working together?"

"If you don't mind. We weren't a bad team."

"No, we weren't," agreed Jake. "Okay, I'll think about it and let you know tomorrow."

"Early."

"Early," promised Jake. "Do you have any information on Kate?"

Gomez eased up out of the chair. "I know she divorced you a couple years back. Once you were gone, Jake, she and I didn't see much of each other. I did get an Xmasfax from her last year."

"Any idea where Dan's going to school down there?"

"None, but we can find out easy enough."

"I've already got somebody working on that."

Gomez moved in the direction of the door. "You might be better off not trying to see her," he suggested. "Of course, coming from a man who's had three wives thus far, this advice may not strike you as that of an expert on how to get along with the ladies."

"Three?"

"Amy and I parted while you were away. I have a new one now. Another blonde—most of my relatives claim they can't tell her from the last one," he said. "Jake, I really hope you'll take this Cosmos thing."

"Early tomorrow—I'll phone you."

Gomez pulled the door open, took a step into the corridor. "About the stuff—go easy, *amigo.*"

"I will. And thanks for getting me out." They shook hands.

"Keep in mind that you've still got a way to go." Giving him a grin and a lazy salute, he took his leave.

Jake returned to the bedroom. He gathered up his Tek gear and stood looking at it. Finally he pushed the bed aside and stashed it all away.

Jake woke up.

It was an interesting, and basically pleasant, experience. And something Jake hadn't done recently.

Yawning, he sat up in bed and stretched.

"It's exactly 9:14 A.M.," announced the voxbox implanted in the side of the bed.

"Thanks for the information."

"Since you didn't leave a wake-up call, the apartment decided to let you sleep until—"

"A wise decision." Jake swung free of the big bed. "Now hush."

"As you wish."

Grinning, Jake barefooted across the room and touched the door of the shower stall. Recognizing his palm print, it slid aside.

"Good morning, Mr. Cardigan. It's April 4, 2120, 9:16 A.M. The outside temperature in the Pasadena Sector of Greater Los Angeles is 67 degrees and—"

"Do something for me," he requested of the stall's voxbox.

"Anything you wish, sir."

"Don't talk to me."

"We're simply doing our best to get you ready in a cheerful way for another stressful day in—"

"Even so." Shedding the pajama top he'd slept in, Jake entered the stall and shut the door.

He scanned the choices on the control panel, decided on a sixty-second warm-water shower and pushed the correct button.

After leaving the alcove, he crossed to his closet. "Most of this stuff is probably out of style by now," he said to himself as the door opened to display his four-year-old-and-more wardrobe. "I should've asked Gomez what's fashionable nowadays—no, forget that. His notions tend to include materials that glow in the dark or cause severe headaches to look at for more than a few seconds."

The bed voxbox said, "Uh . . . hum."

"What?" Jake picked a quiet blue suit.

"We were thinking about preparing your breakfast, sir, but if you're going to continue in this grouchy mood, perhaps you'd rather skip the whole—"

"Tell you what," Jake said. "Put the kitchen on manual."

"Beg pardon?"

"I'll fix my own breakfast. We do have groceries?"

"Of course, sir. They were supplied to the pantry from the condo complex's food warehouse within minutes of your return home."

"Good."

"Uh . . . hum."

"What?"

"Do you mean you want to do *everything?*"

"Sure."

"Including cleaning up afterwards?"

Jake laughed. "I guess you guys can take care of that."

"Thank you, sir."

Dressed, he went down the hall to the small yellow and white kitchen. He was enjoying all the simple rituals of getting up in the morning, he found. Although Jake's life wasn't at one of its high points right now, he basically liked it.

"And it's several notches above the Freezer."

He opened the yellow pantry door, grabbed two of the square

green oranges that they produced up at the Fresno Sector biotech farms.

"I'm going to take the Cosmos job," he said, crouching and looking on the lower kitchen shelves for a plasglass. "First placc, I owe it to Gomez for helping to get me out. And it'll be good to work with him again. Until he showed up last night, I wasn't even certain he hadn't decided I was as crooked as everyone else thinks I am."

"Phone, phone," called the voice of the computer terminal in the living room.

Setting the glass and the cubic oranges on the table, he hurried in to the phone alcove. "Yes?"

"*Buenos días,*" said Gomez, whose curly hair was looking especially lively this morning.

"I've made up my mind," said Jake, sitting and nodding at the phonescreen. "I'm going to take the—"

"I figured you would, *amigo,*" cut in his partner. "Which is why I'm calling you. There's a new development in the Kittridge business and you may as well tag along with me when—"

"Gomez, what is that you're decked out in?"

He glanced down at himself. "A nightshirt."

"Black's a strange color for—"

"Black with *orange* spots. The spots keep it from being morbid. Now if you're all finished heckling my sartorial state—listen to what I have to impart."

"Go ahead, I'm sorry. It's just that I'm not used to seeing things like this so early in the—"

"Late last night," resumed Gomez in a very serious tone, "the Cosmos Agency was contacted by someone who claims to have information about Dr. Kittridge." He glanced to his right, pushed something that was offscreen. "You should now be seeing a still pic of this very person."

The image of a plump, blonde woman of about forty-five appeared on the screen. Her hair was pulled back and she wore a pale blue lab coat. "Who is she?" asked Jake.

"Her name is Dr. Hilda Danenberg and she's a colleague of Dr. Kittridge's at SoCal Tech," answered Gomez, replacing the woman on the screen. "The lady would like to meet at a quiet, out-of-the-way spot. Therefore I've set up a rendezvous for noon today at the Malibu Sector Boardwalk, which has fallen on hard times of late and doesn't attract hordes of patrons. You remember that Brazilian café where we used to have lunch?"

"Sure. Is that still there? Lots of the old places seem to be gone."

"It's still there, except it's a biotech sandwich shop now. The doctor'll be meeting us there in a back booth at the stroke of twelve," he said. "I shall pick you up at the stroke of eleven. Okay?"

"I'll be here and waiting."

"*Muy bien,*" said Gomez. "And I'm tickled beyond measure that you've decided to join up with Cosmos." He paused, glancing offscreen. "Did you enjoy a good night's sleep?"

"I'm not going to use the stuff again. Okay?"

"Okay."

Jake stayed sitting in the alcove for several minutes. "Going to take awhile before even Gomez trusts me completely," he said finally.

It was exactly 10:00 A.M. and Jake was in the Chicano Colony of GLA when the earthquake struck. The cobblestone street began quivering, the two-story imitation-adobe buildings started to shake. A low, angry rumbling went passing under the ground.

Sprinting, Jake got himself positioned in the doorway of Cheena's Mexican Automat. Two red tiles, made of tough plas, came falling down off the slanting roof of the restaurant to land near his feet with a clacking noise.

Someone laughed.

A dark-haired girl of about eleven was riding calmly by on a small electrocycle, grinning at him and shaking her head pityingly. "What an *abuela,*" she observed, laughing at him again and then whizzing off down the bright morning street.

The quake was over and Jake realized that the birds who'd been singing in the decorative trees in the nearby courtyard hadn't even stopped singing during the tremors.

"Apparently," he said to himself as he went on into the restaurant, "I'm overreacting."

The scent of strong spices was thick in the air, mingled with the smells of coffee and chocolate. All along two walls were cubicles covered by plasglass panels, and behind each sat a dish of Mexican food.

A blonde young woman was inserting her Banx card in the slot beneath a cubicle offering a pastry when Jake crossed the threshold.

And a small, dark, chubby man of fifty-six was jumping out of his chair at one of the small round tables across the big room.

Running a zigzag course between the mostly empty tables, Jake reached him before his departure had progressed very far. "Rio," Jake said, disappointment showing in his voice, "I get the impression you want to avoid me."

Rio allowed Jake to urge him back into his chair. "I avoid all minions of the law, Jake."

"I'm not a cop anymore," reminded Jake, sitting and smiling evenly at the plump man. "I'm a convicted felon, remember?"

"Oh, *sí,* that's right." Rio picked up the mug of cocoa he'd been about to abandon and gazed briefly up at the low, stuccoed ceiling. "You've been *dormido.*"

"Want to ask you a few questions," said Jake. "First off, though—why the hell was I the only one who got upset by that earthquake just now? A kid called me a grandmother."

Chuckling, Rio said, "While you were away, *Juanito,* the government of Greater Los Angeles introduced something new—been going on for near to two years. It's a controlled quake plan. Once a week, at ten A.M. in the morning, they let off some pressure and we get a mild quake." He shrugged. "I don't know exactly how they do it, but we haven't had a big one since they started this."

"I better study that booklet Winger gave me."

"Well, it's certainly been great seeing—"

Jake caught Rio's arm, guided him down into a sitting position again. "Only a few more questions."

"Very well. For old time's sake I can— You got to whap it, *señorita.*" He'd noticed the pretty blonde wasn't getting her pastry. "The quakes futz up the mechanism sometimes. Here, allow me to—"

"She'll get it, Rio." Reaching out, Jake caught him.

The blonde dealt the plas door a smack with the heel of her hand and it popped open. "*Gracias,*" she said, smiling over at Rio.

"De nada."

Jake said, "The Cosmos Detective Agency sent—"

"You're working for them now?" He started to rise again.

Jake brought him down with a tug on the sleeve. "They've sent some operatives down into Chihuahua."

"Not a good location to visit just now."

"What happened to them?"

Rio produced a sad sound in his throat. *"Muerto."*

"All three of them are dead?"

Rio held up three fingers, nodding. *"Sí,* it's very sad."

"Who killed them?"

Rio watched the blonde carry her plate to a table. "You don't want to know."

"I do."

"Well, I hear that in two of the deaths it was some important Tek *hombres* who ordered it. I've got no names, so save the next question, Jake."

"Who killed the third one?"

"It was probably Vargas."

"Who's Vargas?"

Rio answered, "He's her present lover, and he doesn't like guys, expecially gringos, trying to get too close to her."

"You're talking about Warbride?"

Rio made a hush motion with his left hand. "It's not smart to talk openly about her hereabouts—or even about Rafe Vargas, for that matter."

Jake said, "A Professor Kittridge and his daughter disappeared down there. Any idea where they are?"

"None." Shaking his head, Rio stood up once more. "But she'd know."

"Warbride?"

After nodding carefully, he started for the door.

A sooty sea gull coughed once, took three lurching steps along the Boardwalk railing, teetered, fell over. Dingy wings flapping awkwardly, it went plummeting straight down to the rubbish-strewn beach twenty feet below. There was a thunk and a rattling when it hit.

Gomez said, "I refuse to take that as an omen." He and Jake were occupying a rusty, green-metal bench about a block away from their upcoming rendezvous spot.

Jake was scanning the area, eyes narrowed slightly in the hazy midday sunlight. "Everything's run down quite a bit hereabouts in the past few years."

The wide, once bright-yellow boardwalk curved along the Malibu Sector coastline for over a mile. On its right side was the Pacific and on its left stood rows of shops, restaurants and saloons. Everywhere paint was peeling, plas-shingles were popped loose, plastiglass windows and doors were streaked with wind-carried beach dirt. Most of the colored pennants that hung on poles along the walkway railing were faded and tattered.

"This Boardwalk got to be quite a tekkie hangout two or so years ago." Gomez checked his watch and then leaned back on the bench. "That led to raids by the GLA cops, our own SCSP, as well as various and sundry anti-Tek agencies. In addition the rival dealers and distributors fought a series of skirmishes—which pitted the Japanese against the Mexicans against the Central Americans against the South Americans against the Africans against the Swiss against the Moonbasers against whoever else was left who was trying to get rich peddling Tek. It was often livelier around here than at a Gomez family reunion."

"Things have been getting worse with Tek?"

Gomez shrugged his left shoulder and grimaced. "In most ways, yes," he said. "There are more rival dealers hustling the stuff, more entrepreneurs trying to manufacture the chips. Use of Tek is up in GLA. Estimates put it at about eighteen percent of the total pop."

"That's up—what?—about five percent?"

Gomez nodded, consulting his watch again. "We've still got near ten minutes before Dr. Danenberg," he announced. "I'm not trying to scare you, Jake, but they've done a lot more research into the stuff while you were away. Did you already know about the possibility of seizures with tekkies? Been more and more of that showing up of late. They call that effect 'kindling,' the formation of a seizure focus. Too frequent use, for some poor bastards anyway, causes them to develop a pretty good imitation of epilepsy. You can get partial complex seizures, which sometimes take the form of flashbacks. Or you might come down with the 'grand mal' version. That's where you shake all over, bite your tongue, lose bladder and bowel control and, if anyone happens to be watching, generally scare the bejabbers out of all and sundry."

"No, most of that wasn't suspected at the time I went up to the Freezer," said Jake. "You've been studying, huh?"

"It was part of my job as a cop," reminded Gomez. "And then, too, since one of my best buddies has Tek for a hobby, why, I figured I ought to learn as much about the stuff as I could. That way we'd have something we could talk about on cold wintry evenings in front of the—"

"I won't be using Tek again."

"Yeah. Seventy-six percent of tekkies promise that at one point or another in their addiction. The percentage that keeps the promise is considerably lower."

Jake started along the Boardwalk. "Time for our meeting, isn't it?"

Gomez paused to button the jacket of his pale yellow suit and took off after him. "Hey, *amigo,* I'm not trying to lecture you," he said, catching up. "But I am concerned."

"I know."

They walked along in silence for a moment.

Then, slowing, Gomez said, "That looks like Dr. Danenberg herself up yonder trying to enter the sandwich shop. Who's that lout blocking her way?"

"Panhandler."

About five hundred yards up ahead the doctor was backing away from a ragged man in an old battle jacket that had BRAZVET written in neon tubing across its back. He was rattling a plascup close to her plump face.

"I'll go dissuade the lad." Gomez started running, dodging the few other strollers on the Boardwalk.

The blonde doctor had retreated to the seaside of the walkway, halting finally with her back against the railing. She was making a go-away motion at the persistent beggar with her right hand.

He reached out, grabbing for her.

She dodged the first lunge, but not the second.

Gomez was just a few hundred feet away from them when the beggar made contact with Dr. Danenberg.

There was all at once an enormous whamming explosion. Fire and swirling black smoke blossomed all around the two figures. The concussion of the blast lifted Gomez right off the planking.

It knocked Jake over, toppling him down hard on his backside.

As he hit, he saw his partner go cartwheeling through the noonday air. Gomez sailed clean over the rail and went falling toward the beach below.

"Jesus." Jake jammed an elbow against the planking, shoved and got himself upright. Stumbling some, he started running for the place where Gomez had gone over.

Jake's foot hit a smear of blackish liquid and he slipped, sliding, nearly falling. He regained his balance, continued running. He noticed there was a scatter of chunks and shards of jagged metal on the walkway, as well as blackened twists of wire and melted scraps of colored plas. But nothing that looked like human remains.

He reached the place where Gomez had gone over. His partner was lying down below on the gritty beach, in a huddled position with his knees and elbows nearly touching. He'd landed on a clear stretch of sand, near the rusted, gutted remains of an old skycar and the innards of an abandoned sofa.

Swinging over the railing, Jake climbed down the understructure of the Boardwalk. There was a dead cat, stiff and grinning, at the spot where he landed.

Two lanky boys of about ten were coming, cautiously, up the beach toward Gomez. Walking close together, both curious and frightened.

Jake sprinted, skirting the debris on the beach, and got to his partner's side. He dropped to one knee, touched his fingertips to Gomez's neck. "Still alive," he said, relieved.

"Some fireworks, *amigo,*" muttered Gomez, eyelids fluttering.

"That they were," agreed Jake. "Just take it easy—there ought to be an ambulance here any minute."

Alarm sirens had been hooting up on the Boardwalk for several minutes now. And, far off, the sirens of a medical van could be heard.

Jake looked up and motioned to the boys, who'd halted about five feet away. "Go on up to the Boardwalk and make sure a medibot gets down here," he said.

The two boys didn't move. Finally the blond one said, "How much?"

"For what?"

"To run an errand for you, mister."

"A dollar."

The dark-haired boy shook his head. "Five bucks or you can forget it."

Jake stood up, rapidly, and pointed at them. "Get your ass up there right now and get help. You'll get your money when you get back here."

The dark-haired one seemed on the brink of arguing, but his companion clutched his arm and yanked him into a run. They started scrambling up the Boardwalk supports.

"I think," said Gomez in a weak, faraway voice, "maybe my leg . . . left one, huh? . . . it's broken."

Jake crouched near him. "It could be—legs don't usually bend this way."

"*Muy tonto.*"

"Who's stupid—me or you?"

"I'm the one . . . should've suspected that . . . bum was a kamikaze."

"He was a *what?*"

Gomez sighed but didn't answer.

Jake leaned closer to his partner. Gomez was still alive, but he'd passed out.

Two white-enameled medibots came down for him a few minutes later.

*

The black plainclothes cop didn't think much of Jake. "Well, it sure didn't take you long to start something, Cardigan," he was saying. "Only your second day off the ice and already you—"

"C'mon, Captain Hambrick. You know damn well I didn't have anything to do with what happened."

"What I know is that Gomez, who was dumb enough to trust you again, is here in the emergency ward." The captain was tall and wide and his voice tended to rumble.

He and Jake were standing in the waiting room of the Emergency Wing of the Pacific Coast Hospital. The green-tinted seethru plastiglass walls looked down on a wide landing/parking area and beyond that a new tract of stilthouses was in the process of being built out over the ocean.

"What's important is Gomez right now." Jake was facing his former Southern California State Police boss. "Our standing here yelling at each other isn't much going to help him."

Outside another skyambulance came chuffing down through the afternoon to the landing area. The rear doors popped open seconds after it touched ground and two medibots eased out carrying a stretcher.

There was a gaunt young woman, her skin pale and bluish and her eyes staring and deeply underscored with shadows, strapped to the stretcher.

"Tekkie," muttered Hambrick, watching them rush her inside the hospital. "Seizure, I'd guess. We can't blame this one on you, though, since you haven't been out long enough to get back into Tek dealing."

The android doctor Jake had talked to fifteen minutes earlier came back into the waiting room through a white swingdoor. He was believably humanoid, only the AND-MD tag he was required by law to wear on his medjacket gave him away.

Jake crossed over to him. "Anything new on Gomez?"

"He's conscious and our robot brainscanners are going over him, Mr. Cardigan. It looks as though Mr. Gomez isn't as seriously injured as we initially estimated."

"That's great. Can I see him?"

"Not just yet, no," said the android doctor, shaking his handsome head. "We have to run quite a few more tests before we can be absolutely certain about your friend's condition."

"What about the head injuries?"

"It will probably turn out to be no more than a concussion." Nodding at Jake and the captain, he went back in to Gomez.

"So you didn't succeed," said Captain Hambrick, "in killing Gomez this time."

Walking away from him, Jake sat on the edge of one of the crimson plastiglass visitors' chairs.

Hambrick sat, grunting some, in the next chair. "While we're waiting for more news, I want to talk to you," he said. "Tell me your version of what happened."

"Tell me something first. That panhandler was an android—but how'd they rig him to kill off Dr. Danenberg?"

"Hell, your Trek-running buddies can explain all that to you. That beggar andy was what they call a kamikaze."

Frowning, Jake said, "So that's what Gomez was trying to tell me—something new to me."

"That's right, you guys don't get to see the vidnews or read a faxpaper up in the Freezer."

"What exactly is the thing?"

"It's a very high class andy," said Hambrick. "We got our first kamikaze killing in GLA just about a year ago. Japan's where they first turned up. They're very expensive, but then Tek runners rarely worry about budgets. These damn andies can pass for humans, as can most of the more expensive andies these days. But the kamikazes can also fool just about any security system—even the most sophisticated ones." He stared out into the afternoon. "Okay, so a kamikaze is instructed to go after a specific target, somebody that one or another of the Tek kingpins wants out of the way. The kamikaze locates his target, quite often in a crowd—which means we're usually likely to get some fringe deaths along with the main hit. The android, which can be a male or female, will just walk right up to the target. Sometimes it pretends to be an old friend, or maybe a tourist who's lost or, as today in the Malibu Sector, a bum looking to get a handout. Then the andy touches the victim—could be a handshake, a pat on a back or even an embrace. Soon as that contact is made there's an explosion. It blows up the victim, the andy and whatever's in the vicinity. Expensive, but impressive."

"Kiss of death," murmured Jake.

"Huh?"

"Reminded me of an old underworld custom I heard about once."

"We've had twenty-seven kamikaze deaths in GLA so far," Hambrick told Jake. "Across the whole country the total is around 264. Over in Japan, where they really love the things, there have been 467 kamikaze murders to date."

"Okay, I know what it is now," said Jake. "But why use it on Dr. Danenberg? Far as I know, she hasn't a damn thing to do with the Tek trade."

Leaning, Hambrick tapped Jake's chest with his forefinger. "Well now, Cardigan, that's just one of the questions I'm hoping you'll answer for me. Oh, and that wasn't actually Dr. Danenberg."

"Another android, wasn't it?"

"Yeah, it was."

"That explains why I didn't see any human remains."

"From what we can determine from the descriptions of the passersby who saw the lady before the blowup—the thing was a simulacrum of the Danenberg woman."

Jake watched a flock of powergliders drifting far out over the ocean, paralleling the hazy horizon. "Why would she have a sim?"

"People use them for lots of reasons. Around here celebs use andy replicas of themselves to stand in at public events, to take their place at a potentially dangerous event or even to handle lectures."

"But this sounds like Dr. Danenberg was expecting an attempt on her life."

"That's one of the assumptions."

"Have you talked to Dr. Danenberg—the real one?"

"We'll certainly do that, soon as we find the lady. She's not at SoCal Tech, not at home and not at several other obvious locations. We're looking for her."

"So what really happened at the Boardwalk was that Gomez risked his life trying to keep one gadget from destroying another gadget."

"That's about it," agreed the captain. "Why were you and Gomez meeting with her?"

"You're going to have to ask the Cosmos Agency about that."

The captain grabbed Jake's arm. "I'm asking you."

Jake took Hambrick's hand from off his sleeve and stood. "I don't work for you anymore."

"Just keep this in mind. As far as I'm concerned you still ought to be on ice," said Captain Hambrick, rising. "You give me too much crap, Cardigan, and I'll do everything I can to see you get sent back to the Freezer."

"I'd figured that out before you even told me."

"I also think you ought to forget about working for Cosmos. You'd be better off trying to find a nice quiet security guard job someplace."

Jake gave him a bleak grin. "This morning maybe I'd have considered quitting. Not now, though—now I'm going to find out who sent that kamikaze."

"That noble bullshit doesn't impress me," said Hambrick. "You've always been a cold, calculating son of a bitch—that's why they all called you the Android. Listen, if Gomez was lying in there dead now, you really wouldn't give a damn. So don't pretend—"

"You bastard!" Jake's fist went back and he started to throw a punch. But then he stopped. Shaking his head, he dropped his hands to his sides and stepped back. "No, nope. I'm not going to let you goad me into hitting you, Captain. You're not going to get me back up to the Freezer that easy."

Hambrick laughed without opening his mouth. Giving Jake a disdainful look, he turned and walked away.

Jake stood watching him until Hambrick was outside. He worked hard to get his anger under control. That took several minutes.

The beautiful silver-skinned and platinum-haired receptionist said, "I'm not an android."

"I'll keep that in mind." Jake was sitting in a licorice-colored plastiglass chair in the Tower II reception room of the Cosmos Detective Agency Building.

"What I'm getting at is, I'm a human being," she added, tapping a finger against her silvery cheek. "I've been going through some what you might call changes in my life lately and I decided to experiment with my basic *look.*"

"It's striking."

"This is only my second day with the new makeup approach," she said. "But so far three clients have confused me with the servomechs and a new 'bot on the custodial staff tried to dust and polish me."

"There is a sort of mechanical aura."

"The trouble is, see, you can't just take the stuff off. You have to go have it done at the same salon where they slapped it on in the first place."

"You considering doing that already?"

"I am, except right now I can't afford having it taken off, since I haven't even finished paying for having it put on," she explained. "You're the one who's a friend of Gomez, aren't you?"

"We're friends, yes."

"How is he? I just heard about his getting himself hurt."

"He's doing fine—except for the broken leg."

"That's good news."

"Send him in, Marny," said the emerald-green voxbox sitting atop her stark white desk.

Marny pointed at the box and mouthed the words, "That's Bascom." She next pointed at a white door across the room. "You can go in now, Mr. Cardigan."

Grinning, Jake left the chair and crossed to the door.

Walt Bascom's office was large and cluttered. Its walls were made of blind plastiglass that showed nothing of the Laguna Sector outside.

Bascom was a small, compact man of fifty-five, sunbrown and clad in an expensive and considerably rumpled suit. He was seated on top of a lucite desk in the middle of the office, cross-legged, noodling on a wheezy alto saxophone. There were piles of faxcopies, files, memos of many colors, printout sheets, summonses and assorted paper ephemera surrounding him on the clear desktop. Steepled over a stack of final-notice bills was a yellowed booklet titled *BeBop Favorites of the 20th Century.*

Jake wended his way through the sprawl of folders, bundles of papers, weapons, discarded clothes and abandoned dishware that lay between him and his new employer.

"I did," said Bascom as he set aside the saxophone.

"Did what?"

"Slept in my clothes—you were probably wondering if I had."

"I already knew you had. It's one of your trademarks." Jake took a plascarton of old lazguns off a tinchair, brushed off the accumulated dust with the pair of paisley panties that were beneath the carton and sat down, uninvited. "Did some research on you earlier in the day."

"That's only fair—since I've been researching you for several weeks." Bascom wore his graying hair close cropped. After knuckling the top of his head, he commenced rummaging the piles of material on his desk. "How's Gomez doing?"

"Well."

Bascom opened the folder. "Jonathan Cardigan, Jr.," he read from the topmost sheet of faxpaper. "You've been described as—insubordinate, sarcastic, irreverent, cynical, unpatriotic, disrespectf—"

"Maybe you shouldn't have sprung me."

"I trust Gomez. He says you're okay."

Jake leaned back in the chair. "And besides you don't have anybody else who can get safely through Warbride's territory," he said. "You've already had three Cosmos operatives killed down there."

"One killed." The agency chief held up his forefinger. "Other two are simply missing."

"All three of them are dead and gone. That's another thing I found out this morning."

Bascom scratched his head. "Gomez mentioned you had good sources of information," he said. "Seems you really do—either that or you're conning me."

"I quit lying at job interviews my second year in college," Jake assured him. "I'm fairly sure I can handle this assignment alone, since Gomez is laid up. I'll get through to the crash site in the *Selva Grande* and I'll determine if the Kittridges are dead or alive. If you still want to hire me, now that Gomez can't team up with me, then fine. But don't lecture me about my many failings. I've already got Captain Hambrick to take care of that."

"Hold off, Cardigan." Bascom held up one hand. "You haven't allowed me to get to the part where I inform you that I actually, within reason, like fellows who're insubordinate, sarcastic, irreverent and the rest. Particularly fellows of that ilk who know their way around down across the border." Hopping free of his desk, he stood facing Jake. "If you want the job, it's yours."

"Yeah, I do want it."

Bascom, smoothing at some wrinkles in his trousers, worked his way over to a four-foot-wide hologram projection stage. He sidearmed the folders stacked there off onto the rug. "Can you see from where you're perched?"

Jake raised off his chair, moved aside the disabled bartender robot that had been in his line of vision and sat again. "Just fine."

On all fours, the head of the Cosmos Detective Agency searched around on the floor. "Ah, here she is." He'd located the hologram cartridge he was after and, smiling, held it up toward Jake before inserting it in the base slot.

Upon the stage there appeared a life-size, full-dimensional image of Beth Kittridge. She was sitting in a lemon-yellow rattan chair, smiling at someone to her left and carrying on an unheard conversation. Her dress was of dark green neorayon.

Jake stood, moving closer to the projection stage. He was feeling an odd constriction across his chest.

"Something?" inquired Bascom, glancing over at him.

"Nothing, no." He returned to the chair, trying to remember where he'd seen her before.

"This is Beth Kittridge," explained Bascom. "Our footage was taken three months ago during a reception at SoCal Tech for a few scientific gents who were visiting from the Moon Colony." He circled the platform. "According to our sources, she still wears her hair like this—long, down to the shoulders. A pretty young woman, if you like them on the slender side. You obviously find her attractive."

"Do I?"

"Well, Cardigan, when a fellow jumps up, clicks his heels together and lets his tongue unfurl a foot or two—an astute detective such as myself deduces there's an interest."

Jake grinned. "Okay, she's attractive."

"Agreed. But don't let that foul up your investigation. And keep in mind that all you may find down there is the young lady's corpse."

"Yeah, I know."

Beth was suddenly gone from the stage, replaced by her father. He was standing, leaning against a section of neosteel railing and apparently conversing with someone out of camera range.

"Same reception," said Bascom as he made another circuit of the hologram stage. "Supposedly Dr. Kittridge has lost approximately ten pounds since then and will appear even leaner than—"

"Why the weight loss?"

"We don't know." Bascom sat on the edge of the stage, merging with part of the image. "Could've been ill-health, worry or something else again."

"Any of which might tie in with what happened to him down in Mexico."

"Dr. Danenberg might know, but she remains among the missing." He rose up and away from the stage. "Another fellow I want you to observe . . ." Kittridge vanished and was replaced by the image of a good-looking blond man of about forty. "Here we have—"

"Bennett Sands," supplied Jake.

"You know him?"

Jake replied, "My wife—my former wife—worked for Sands for a while as a sort of private secretary and girl Friday. That was right before I went up to the Freezer. And for a while thereafter, I think."

"She worked for him fourteen months all told."

Jake said, "Then you knew I knew who he was."

"Forgive me for being tricky when I don't even have to be." Bascom started another slow circle of the stage. "Sands remains a multimillionaire and the director of BioFoods, Inc. His late father it was who came up with the exclusive tissue-culture bioprocess system that allows BioFoods to manufacture what I still think of as artificial real food—meat, vegetables, whatever. They have plants and headquarters all over the world—and on the Moon."

"When Kate—when my ex-wife—worked for Sands he was based in GLA."

"He operates out of Mexico nowadays," said the Cosmos chief. "We believe that Kittridge was involved with Sands in some way and may even have been en route to visit him in one of his Mexican hideaways when the crash occurred."

"What does Sands say?"

"We haven't been able to locate him since the Kittridges, father and daughter, disappeared."

The stage made a clicking sound and Sands was gone.

"This case," said Jake. "We're really not talking just about a simple insurance claim, are we?"

Bascom busied himself with extracting the cartridge and then hunting for a place to set it. "What makes you say that?"

"For one thing, someone just tried to kill Dr. Danenberg when they suspected she was going to pass information on to us," he said. "It could be that the Kittridge heirs are a violent bunch and they want to make sure they collect the insurance money. But I somehow doubt that."

"The beneficiaries under the Moonbase-Hartford policy are Kittridge's two sisters. One's married and lives in Seattle; one's divorced and resides in Paris. Neither one is in need of money, and their activities over the past two weeks don't tie them in with Dr. Kittridge or his daughter in any way."

"Okay, then who is it who's taking such an interest in Kittridge?"

Putting both hands behind his back, Bascom stared up at his off-white ceiling. "Well, there are a few others who may be interested in the present whereabouts of the doctor."

"Such as who?"

"I can't provide a complete list of names just yet," said Bascom. "Though I'd certainly include Sonny Hokori."

Jake stood. "Hokori—what's a small-time Tek dealer got to do with Kittridge?"

"Hokori's come a long way since you tangled with him four years ago, Cardigan. Fact is, he's just about the top man in the business right now."

Jake made his way over to the agency chief. "Is that why you're really hiring me—because you think I was working for Hokori back then? That I got the investigation of him and his bosses killed?"

"No, I agree with Gomez that you never worked for Sonny Hokori—and that you were framed."

"Hokori doesn't owe me any favors, if that's—"

"You're not paying attention. Calm down and listen," advised the compact detective. "I mentioned Hokori because he's maybe involved in the Kittridge case. And also I figure you might want another chance at the fellow. Okay?"

Jake took a deep breath, let it out slowly. "Yeah, okay," he said. "How do they tie together?"

"Supposedly Dr. Kittridge has been doing research on an anti-Tek device," said Bascom. "Details on its exact nature are fuzzy, but quite a few people seem to believe that he's succeeded in coming up with a gadget that can—well, neutralize Tek chips and render them useless. That would have a very negative effect on the future fortunes of Sonny Hokori and his colleagues."

"How's his system work?"

Bascom shook his head. "We're still digging into that aspect of this business," he said. "But the fact that Kittridge has apparently perfected this thing means we're not the only ones who're interested in what's become of him."

"It could be that Sonny had him killed—and that the crash wasn't an accident."

"There's also the possibility that Dr. Kittridge had his anti-Tek device and his notes on it with him," said Bascom. "Giving several folks a motive for locating that wreckage."

"Did Gomez know about the Tek angle?"

"Not yet. I was intending to brief both of you this afternoon."

"Maybe if you'd briefed him yesterday he wouldn't be in the hospital now."

"Maybe," admitted Bascom.

"Any other items you've held back?"

"Nary a one," swore Bascom, working his way back through the clutter to his desk. "I've worked out a sort of an itinerary for you—for the first part of your investigation, anyway." He had to search through only three folders before finding the sheet of yellow paper he wanted. "You can't, obviously, go directly to the crash site. So we're routing you into Mexico by way of the Borderland. You'll stop there and contact the Mexican Federal Police. Get from them whatever they have on the Kittridge crash."

"Won't be much more than you already have."

"True, but it's a formality we have to go through—makes the cops on both sides of the border happy," said the Cosmos chief. "After that, Cardigan, you're going to be pretty much on your own. I'll supply you with your contacts down there, but you're going to want to use your own, too. What you have to do is arrange yourself safe conduct to the scene of the Kittridge accident. Keep in mind that we're not supposed to be interested in the anti-Tek aspects of the case. We get our fee for establishing whether the Kittridges are dead or alive. That's all."

Nodding, Jake said, "Finding Kittridge's anti-Tek device might earn a bonus from someplace, though."

"That's very true, but just don't get yourself killed trying for it. In fact, officially I can't encourage you in the anti-Tek direction at all." He leaned across his desk and held out his hand. "The starting salary, by the way, is seventy-five thousand dollars a year. Is that satisfactory?"

"For a start." Jake shook hands and left the office.

The day was ending when he reached the street level. He walked across to an aircab stand and got into the only one there, a fairly new scarlet one.

"Where to?" inquired the robot cabbie.

"Pasadena Sector." Jake gave him his condo address.

"Here we go." The cab shuddered once, then rose up into the gathering twilight.

But instead of heading inland for the Pasadena Sector, it turned southward and down the coast.

"You're flying the wrong direction," warned Jake.

"That's only your opinion."

Jake eased out his lazgun. "Land this thing right about now," he suggested to the robot cabbie. "Otherwise I'll disable you and take over myself."

"I got to warn you," said the robot as the aircab flew southward through the dusk, "that I'm not your usual mechanical cabbie. You use that gun on me—or even make a jab at me with a screwdriver—and we're both in the soup."

With the barrel of his weapon pointing at the back of the mechanical man's skull, Jake asked, "How so?"

"They got me rigged to explode—and I mean with a big bang—if I get diddled with in any way."

"Drastic."

"Whoever it is wants to see you, they want to see you bad."

"Who might that be?"

The cabbie's head rattled slightly when he gave it a negative shake. "That information I don't possess."

"What's our destination?"

"The Anaheim Sector."

Off to the right the Pacific was growing darker as the sun dropped further below the horizon.

Jake moved the gun down to rest on his knee.

After a moment the robot inquired, "You going to attempt any violence?"

"Not just yet."

The wreck of a huge interplanetary spaceship was lying on its side in a stretch of pocked wasteland directly below in the deepening twilight.

The aircab dropped down through the dusk, skimming under a high, wide, rust-spattered arch that the words SPACELAND PARK spelled out across it in dead lighttubing. The cab touched ground, skimmed and skittered for several hundred feet, then settled down about a quarter of a mile from the wrecked ship.

"I'm not used to landing on a Martian desert," apologized the robot cabbie.

"This amusement park's been out of business for ten—make that fourteen years."

"Nevertheless this is where they rigged me to deliver you."

The passenger door popped open.

Gun in hand, Jake climbed out into the new night.

"No hard feelings." The cab huffed a few times, shimmied, went climbing up and away across the fresh darkness.

A tumbled-over metal sign to Jake's right read—SPEND 15 MINUTES ON MARS! JUST 3 TICKETS!

Far across the simulated Martian landscape Jake noticed a pack of about a half dozen wild dogs foraging and fighting.

"Only sign of life," he remarked to himself and started hiking in the direction of the fallen spacecraft a quarter of a mile away.

Dust swirled up around his boots as he walked.

When he was still several hundred yards from the wreck, lights went on inside the sprung-open doorway.

Jake slowed, brought up his gun.

A faint electric buzzing started up inside the fallen spaceship.

There was a faint wind and it came blowing across the night

desert, scattering dust and tatters of paper. One of the wild dogs howled.

"Come on in, Jake. This isn't an ambush," invited a voice from inside the ship.

Jake kept his gun raised and ready as he climbed inside. There were two floating globe lights in the rusted husk of what had once been the ship's control cabin.

Seated in a canvas chair was a handsome tanned man of forty-five. He was wearing a sky-blue fakesilk suit and was completely bald. Tattooed on the left side of his polished scalp was one bright-crimson rosebud. "Did you have a pleasant nap up in the Freezer, my boy?" he asked.

"You're coming in a bit blurred, Winterguild," observed Jake. "Your hologram remote projector needs tuning."

"You're the first to complain," said Kurt Winterguild, smiling faintly.

"Still in business, huh?"

"As a matter of fact, my boy, I've risen in the International Drug Control Agency since you went into hibernation," said the tattooed man. "I'm now Field Director for the Western United States."

"We always knew you'd rise in your chosen profession. Congratulations." Jake tucked his lazgun into his waistband. "Did you invite me out here to help you celebrate your promotion?"

"I was anxious for a private talk," said the IDCA agent, crossing his legs. "What I'd really like to see you do, Jake, is forget all about Dr. Kittridge."

"Oh, so?"

"My agency is handling the matter and—"

"Handling it how? You hunting for the doctor?"

"Even as we speak, Jake, I'm here in Mexico, heading up the search."

"Meaning you don't know where he and his daughter are?"

"We're not actually that interested in Beth Kittridge—only insofar as she might be able to tell us where her father is if we found her."

"Did he have it with him?"

"Did he have what, my boy?"

"His anti-Tek device?"

Winterguild laughed. "Not exactly."

"But he has something you want."

"We want Dr. Kittridge himself, Jake."

"Before Sonny Hokori gets him."

"Before anyone, you included, locates him."

"So the crash was real?"

Winterguild laughed again, recrossed his legs. "Ah, four years on ice hasn't modified you much, my boy. You still try to get more than give." He rested his elbow on his knee, leaned toward Jake and gave him a searching gaze. "I'm requesting that you drop the Kittridge investigation."

"Walt Bascom'd be the one I'd take that sort of request up with—were I you."

"Our feelings have already been conveyed to him."

"Yeah, and I can guess what he told you. Which saves me from telling you."

"Reflect on my suggestions, Jake. I really don't want to have to worry about your intruding in my investigation," Winterguild said. "Keep in mind, too, my boy, that there can be a lot worse things than a stay in the Freezer."

"And you keep in mind that if I ever meet up with something other than a projection of you—watch out."

Laughing once again, the drug agent vanished and left Jake alone in the dark.

The slim, deeply tanned man took a pack of marihuana cigarettes out of his jacket pocket. "Smoke, Jake?"

Jake shook his head. "No thanks, Jerry."

It was a few minutes after six in the evening and they were sitting in candy-striped plaschairs beside a large oval swimming pool. Beyond the pool rose an impressive Moroccan-style mansion, rich with wrought-iron and bright red tiles, surrounded with thick foliage and bright flowers. This was in the exclusive Watts Sector.

"You implied on the phone I might be able to help you," said Jerry Sundell. "Is it about a job? Because, much as I'd like to honor our old, deep friendship, Jake buddy, Sundell Productions isn't as vast as it was before you—"

"I'm not looking for a job in the porno industry."

Sundell lit his cigarette and then laughed. "Hey, I'm out of porno, Jake. Have been for three years, ever since the Supreme Court/West Coast Division ruled that showing sexual intercourse between life-like androids was as filthy and obscene as when humans screw." He sighed out smoke. "It ruined pornography as we know it."

"What are you producing now?"

"Legitimate vidwall movies. In fact, I may be able to use you as a consultant on one of them. It's going to be about the Tek Wars."

"Tek Wars?"

"You know, the battles between the various Tek interests, the battles with the various anti-Tek government agencies. It's, I'm telling you, Jake buddy, the stuff of high drama and excitement." He leaned forward in his chair. "The movie will also have romance, a terrific subplot and lots of bimbos with impressive tits."

"During that earlier phase of your career, you knew some important people in the Tek trade."

"Only casually."

"And you still have some contacts."

"Not really, no. I mean, I'm making an important film attacking the bastards. I couldn't still be—"

"Camouflage," said Jake quietly. "What do you know about Leon Kittridge?"

"Not much."

"If you're producing this Tek epic, you have to know about—"

"Jake, I'm commencing to be a bit offended." Sundell stood up, tossed his marihuana cigarette into the pool. After its sizzle had faded, he added, "What I mean is, I'm a movie exec of substance now, a major vidwall producer. To come here and imply that—Oh, shit!"

Jake turned to look at what the producer was staring at.

The entire impressive mansion was starting to shimmer and shake.

"Another quake?" asked Jake.

"Shit, goddamn it, shit."

The wrought-iron trim faded, grew dim and was gone. Next the thick, cream-colored stucco walls blurred and disappeared.

In less than three minutes the entire vast house had vanished. A foundation and the floors and some furniture was all that remained. In what had been the master bedroom a naked redheaded young woman sat up in the oval bed and scowled over at Sundell.

"You putz," she accused.

"Honey, I swear to God I paid the bill to Habitex, Inc."

"Schlep," she yelled. "This is really frigging embarrassing."

"Honey, I'll phone them right now to complain. The house'll be back in less than an hour."

"What was the house?" asked Jake. "A hologram projection?"

"Yeah, yeah. It's a hell of a lot cheaper than actually building. This part of the Watts Sector is very much sought after and the lot alone set me back a million, four hundred thousand," the unsettled producer explained. "So when Habitex, Inc., suggested a big socko house for just three thousand a month, I took it."

"You behind on the rent?"

"Naw, not really. Only four months."

"The epics aren't paying?"

"Not as well as porno did," Sundell admitted. "Now, Jake, I really have to—"

"Tell me what you know about Kittridge first," suggested Jake, getting a persuasive grip on his nearest arm. "Tell me what you've heard from your contacts in the Tek trade."

"All right. What I know is this, Jake buddy—this Kittridge was onto something, something that can foul up the business. A lot of them wanted Kittridge to give up what he was working on."

"So they killed him?"

"I'm not sure, some of them only wanted to talk to him. Maybe negotiate something, you know."

"Was Sonny Hokori one of those involved?"

"Him especially," said Sundell. "Now, Jake, I really have to get—oh, shit!" He was staring up into the twilight sky, deepening sadness showing on his evenly tanned face.

A skyvan was chuffing down, obviously intending to land on his property. Emblazoned across its underbelly in glowing neon was SEXIANDIES/RENTALS & REPAIRS.

"You schlub," called the naked redhead. "You haven't even kept up the payments on *me!*"

"Jake, can we continue this another time maybe?"

"Sure, Jerry, and thanks." Jake started for the place where the gate to the street had been.

Jake double-timed up the steps of the Library/Social Centre that rose up in the exact middle of the SoCal Tech college campus. The wide plasdoors wooshed open for him and he entered the multi-floored lobby.

Students and a scattering of teachers were moving along the various walkramps, some aiming upward toward the voxbooks floor, others making their way down to the VidEd levels. Just to the right of the information desk a Prof Smartz robot sat in a plas armchair. Chrome-plated—his humanoid face reminding Jake of Winger—and husky, the 'bot wore a tweedy jacket and gray slacks. He was smoking a pipe and gazing intently at the slim young woman student who'd just inserted her Banx card in the slot in his pedestal. Just below the slot a plas placque announced—*This is a licensed Prof Smartz (C)2118 by EdAid,Ltd. One of 162,000 serving universities and colleges around the world. For Service call Arcade Ent,Oxnard Sector,GLA.*

"Still researching the Greenhouse Effect, Lana?" the robot asked her in his warm, avuncular voice.

"Yes, Prof, I need some more stuff on the Great Forest plan and how it's policed," she told the seated robot. "But, listen, I can't afford more than a hundred dollars of info this week."

Prof Smartz winked. "Well, we can slip you a little extra on the side, dear."

Jake reminded himself he had a date and moved on.

An upslanting ramp had an arrow and the words STUDENT/FACULTY DRINKING AREA imbedded in its slick surface.

He started up the ramp.

Jake stopped just inside the silver-beaded curtain that masked the entryway to the High Technology Saloon. It was a few minutes past ten in the evening, and every light in the New Hollywood Sector of Greater Los Angeles could be seen glittering far below the curving viewalls of the crowded tower bar.

Down at the far end of the long chrome and ivory bar Jake spotted the pretty Chinese young woman he'd come here to meet.

A pudgy man in a candystriped suit was sitting too close to her, swaying on his ebony stool and steadying himself by clutching at her nearest knee.

Smiling in a seemingly cordial way, she touched his temple with the ring finger of her right hand.

The pudgy man sat suddenly upright, looking surprised in the few seconds before he toppled over facefirst into the bowl of soypretzels in front of him on the ivory bar.

"What'd you do to him, Patricia?" asked Jake as he stopped at her side.

Continuing to smile, Pat Wong showed him the simple silver ring. "Low-grade stunner. I worked it up myself. It won't keep him out for more than an hour or so," she explained. "It's good to see you again, Jake."

"Remind me not to fondle you."

She eased off the stool. "There's a table over there for us."

"Leaving him here?"

"Good a place as any. I don't like to be approached by strangers," Pat said. "How are you doing?"

Following her to a chrome and ebony table, Jake answered, "I'm actually feeling not bad."

She smiled. "That sounds a trifle better than rotten."

He sat opposite her. "I need some information."

"So I figured from your call. What sort of information do you need?"

"You're still writing for *Electronics Week* and teaching part-time at SoCal Tech."

"I'm in the same rut, yes. I've changed less than anyone while you were away."

"I'm working for the Cosmos Agency now and—"

"With Gomez—you make a good team."

"Except he's sidelined."

"I heard about that. You weren't hurt?"

"A few bruises," he replied. "We were assigned to find Dr. Kittridge and his daughter, Beth. Any idea about what happened to them?"

"They crashed, down in Mexico. Week or so ago."

"What information do you have about that?"

"Only what came into the magazine by way of AP/MEX."

Jake rested an elbow on the table. "What about their reasons for traveling down—"

"Each guest is required to order a drink within five minutes of arrival," reminded the table's voxbox in a cultured and polite voice.

Jake looked across at Pat. "Still drinking the same thing?"

"The rut is all-encompassing."

"Two dark ales," he told the table.

It whirred and two compartments opened in its dark top. Two glasses of ale popped up.

Jake ignored his. "About Kittridge?"

"About eleven months ago Leon took a leave from SoCal Tech," Pat said, running a fingertip along the frosted side of her glass. "He started working in the lab he had in their home in the Woodland Hills Sector. I heard, though, that there's also a laboratory someplace down across the border. I'm not sure where that one is. Beth has been working at home with him on his private project. I can't confirm this next, but supposedly Bennett Sands is financing him—in part at least."

"Sands again," said Jake. "What are the Kittridges working on?"

"Kittridge has had two major interests. Robotics—specifically the building of superandroids, ones that can pass for human in every way. His other interest, a more recent one, has been to come up with a way to stop Tek. A brother of his, the ne'er-do-well that most families have at least one of—I'm the one in the local Wong clan. This brother died from using the stuff three years ago—a seizure."

Jake tapped his fingers on the tabletop. "They say Kittridge has succeeded."

"Who says?"

"My boss for one," he replied. "This anti-Tek device—any notion what it is?"

"It involves RF waves—radio frequency waves emitted at a high oscillation rate," said Pat. "At least, that's what I suspect—based on various hints and clues I've pieced together. As yet I don't have enough to try a piece for the magazine."

"How'd you use that on Tek chips?"

She smiled at him. "Well, Jake, if you could set up just the right oscillation rate—you could shatter the chip."

"How many of them at once?"

"If you worked it right—if you, say, broadcast your special high-frequency RF by way of a satellite setup—you ought to be able to access every single Tek chip on the globe at once. Maybe those on the Moon and in the various orbiting colonies, too."

"Access and destroy them?"

"That's it."

"Christ." He picked up his glass of dark ale and drank some. "It's easy to see why several people are interested in finding Dr. Kittridge."

"Somebody you really ought to talk to is Hilda Danenberg."

"That's what Gomez and I tried to do earlier in the day, Pat."

"I know, Jake."

"That simulacrum android of Dr. Danenberg—was that one of Kittridge's?"

"A joint effort. He and Hilda worked together on the andies," answered Pat. "And, initially, she helped him on the anti-Tek work, too. But once Kittridge got close to achieving his goal, he and Hilda parted company. That happened about a month or so ago."

"Was there a romance, too?"

Nodding, she drank some of her ale. "More on her side than his, however."

"Would she be likely to try to kill him? Out of anger at being—"

"No, Hilda doesn't work that way. She'd be much more likely to consult a team of good attorneys and sue the man."

"Any idea where she might be hiding out?"

"Across the border. She went down there a lot, with Kittridge and alone."

Jake sipped his ale. "If Bennett Sands is financing the anti-Tek research—what's he get out of it?"

"He sells it to the government when it's perfected. Don't even bother about the possibility of his planning to donate it to the world. Your wife didn't tell you much about Sands, did she?"

"Not a lot, no. Mostly because I never asked."

"You should've, Jake."

"Why?"

"Because he isn't exactly a decent man. He's in this simply out of greed, which is never a very admirable motive."

"Do you know where he is?"

"He has places all over—even a villa on the Moon." Finishing her ale, she leaned back. "Be very careful," Pat cautioned. "Something could happen to you—even worse than what happened to Gomez."

"So I've been told."

Jake sat straddling the white chair. He'd just given Gomez a concise account of what he'd found out during the day. "A lot more than insurance seems to be involved," he concluded.

His injured partner was propped up in the wide white bed. His left leg was uncovered and in a white plasticast for about two-thirds of its length.

"Okay, there's another obvious possibility that seems to be lurking behind the facts here." Gomez's curly hair was somewhat subdued tonight. "It must've occurred to you."

"The possibility that Dr. Kittridge and his daughter aren't dead—and didn't even crash."

"Yeah, that the crash is a fake."

"Rigged by who?"

"Could be the Kittridges themselves."

Jake nodded. "To throw off the Tek kingpins who are anxious to halt their researches."

"Or, *amigo,* they may want to elude Bennett Sands. He contributes millions to the perfecting of the anti-Tek gimmick. Then Dr. Kittridge appears to die. A few months later another scientist entirely introduces his anti-Tek gimmick and reaps all the profits. He's a front for Kittridge, but Sands doesn't know that. You're making forlorn faces. You don't like this scenario?"

"I don't, even though it's plausible."

"You object because it would mean Beth Kittridge is a party to a fraud—and you don't want to believe she's capable of anything like that."

"Her father could've faked the crash without telling her about it in advance."

"She's supposed to be smart. Wouldn't she be likely to inquire—'Gloriosky, Daddy, whyever are we landing here in the middle of this great big old forest instead of at the goddamn airport?' "

Jake said, "Another obvious possibility, with Sonny Hokori involved, is that they were shot down deliberately. And are dead."

"Just as likely that he waylaid their skycruiser and grabbed them," suggested his partner. "Because there's another interesting possibility to this electronic Passover the doctor and his daughter have been planning. If that comes off, then all the Tek in the universe is going to go blooey." He held up a forefinger. "But maybe not Sonny's. Not Sonny's if he gets Dr. Kittridge to provide *his* Tek chips with a defense against this high-frequency stuff."

"Sure—that way Hokori would have a global monopoly on Tek," said Jake. "In a way, I hope he is involved in this. I'd like to meet him again."

"Revenge can be tricky," cautioned his partner.

"You've got to depart, Mr. Cardigan," the nurse said and withdrew.

Jake stood up and said, "I'll be leaving for the Borderland early tomorrow."

"Good luck, *amigo,*" said Gomez. "I hope you find them alive."

The Borderland was a vast, miles-wide strip of land that ran between the United States and Mexico and stretched along the border from California as far as Texas. A wide-open territory, it was governed by Mexico and attracted tourists from all across the world.

Las Cruces was as freewheeling as any of the Borderland towns, and when Jake arrived there early in the afternoon all its many streetlights were full on, glaring, blinking, flashing and offering hundreds of bright-colored invitations and temptations. There were also dozens of huge vidscreens, animated adwalls, triop billboards and hologram teasers.

Through the dust-streaked plaswindows of the landcab he'd taken from the airport he saw a succession of hotels, cafés, cantinas, gambling joints, sports pavilions, bordellos and souvenir shops—PACO'S POKER PALACE, CRAPSHOOTERS' CLUB DELUXE, MOVIE MUSEUM BORDELLO—SLEEP WITH ANDY REPLICAS OF YOUR FAVORITE STARS PAST & PRESENT!, ROOSTER FIGHT STADIUM, CASA DEL BINGO, MAMA LAVIDA'S NATURAL BORDELLO—LIVE HOOKERS ONLY!, WRESTLING HALL—STRONGMEN VS. ROBOTS!

"Here's something that hasn't changed much in four years," he said to himself.

"*Caramba!*" exclaimed the robot cabbie. "We are arrive, *señor*." He was copper colored and his costume consisted of just a multicolored serape and a tasseled sombrero.

The landcab rattled, gave out a few moderate explosive sounds and thunked to a stop in front of the Paloma Hotel, a narrow ten-story structure of glass, silvery metal and adobe.

Jake dropped the proper amount of pesos into the meterbox in front of him and picked up his single suitcase. "*Gracias*," he said.

"Allow me, *señor,* to ask of you a question, *por favor*."

Jake halted halfway out. "Sure."

"Have I struck you as sufficiently picturesque, as colorful enough?"

"More than enough."

"I'm one of the new models the company is trying out. I'd like to get the tourist reaction."

Jake climbed all the way out of the cab. "Well, they just might want to run a few more tests. *Adiós*." He made his way into the hotel and checked in.

Captain Ernest Manzano was not in uniform. A long, lean and sad-faced man of forty, he was wearing a faded blue warm-up suit. His office, in one of the underground wings of the Mexican Federal Police Building, was large and smelled faintly of damp earth. He was sitting behind his carved wood desk in a slumped position, and he didn't become any more animated when he noticed that Jake had entered. "Tell me this, Jake," he said. "Why waste your time over a couple of missing tourists? Down on this side of the border people are vanishing all the time. It's easier just to let them stay that way."

Sitting in a rattan chair facing the desk, Jake said, "It's comforting to see you're as enthusiastic as ever, Ernie."

"Detective work is only a job. I can never convince you of that."

"My job right now is to find out what happened to Dr. Kittridge and his daughter."

"I know, I know—and you're obliged to pay me a token visit."

"Actually, Ernie, despite what you pretend, you're not a bad cop."

"My one flaw is that I keep letting myself get interested in some of these cases and some of these people," the captain admitted. "It's a very bad habit."

"What do you know about the Kittridges?"

Sighing, Manzano lifted himself up. Both he and the chair creaked. "You're not the only one looking for them, Jake."

"Winterguild is hunting—who else?"

"Winterguild." Manzano chuckled. He drifted over to a computer terminal, slouching down into the chair that faced its stand. "I know some of Sonny Hokori's men were trying to slip across the border into the state of Chihuahua recently. And Raoul Martinez's goons are interested in the whereabouts of the good doctor as well."

"Martinez still in Tek?"

"Very much so. We just closed down—closed down by blowing the damn thing sky-high—a *maquiladora* he had off in the wilds near here. A *maquiladora* is a small factory that once—"

"I know, Ernie. I can also count up to ten in Spanish."

"*Por supuesto.* I forgot that you're not a *gringo*," said Manzano as he languidly touched the computer key pad.

A three-dimensional simulation formed on the screen, showing a stretch of forestland. The trees were huge, trunks thick and wide, and the topmost branches were hundreds of feet above the ground.

"Is this the *Selva Grande* where the skycruiser went down?" Jake went over to stand behind the captain and look down at the screen.

Manzano touched a few more keys. "This is where the Kittridges allegedly crashed. You'll notice that the spot is conveniently close to one of the main roadways cutting through the forest. And not far from this . . ."

A ranger station appeared on the computer screen. It consisted of a spacious adobe and red-tile ranchhouse and a metal-fretted tower of several hundred feet.

"Still no word from this place?"

"Nothing from either station since your *querida* Warbride took over."

"Sweetheart isn't the word I'd use to describe—"

"Nor I actually, but I'm striving to maintain my polite public-relations persona, Jake. So I stay clear of words like *puta*."

"How strong is she?"

"You mean would it be better to wait until the state falls again into federal hands?"

"Yeah. I'm curious as to how long you think she'll hold on to control."

"Quite a while." Manzano raised his left hand almost shoulder high and fluttered it. "The Mexican government is not in great shape just now. They won't be able to come up with troops or funds to combat her—and your own government is holding off on committing any kind of support. Chihuahua is going to be run by Warbride for a time, and the lady may even branch out. She's popular and she's smart. So, Jake; if you want to visit the woods—you've got to do it with her blessing."

"Do you think Warbride's directly involved with whatever happened to the Kittridges?"

The captain leaned back in his chair. "I don't think anything could've happened to them over there without her knowing about it."

"Even an accident?"

"An arranged accident, *sí*."

"Where do you think they were heading?"

"Probably to see a *gringo* named Bennett Sands. You know of him, don't you?"

Jake laughed. "C'mon, Ernie. You know my wife used to work for Sands."

"*Naturalmente*—it slipped my mind for a moment. Dr. Kittridge and his daughter have visited Sands several times over the past year. He owns a villa and plantation at the far border of Chihuahua."

"Is he tied up with what happened?"

"Most people consider him to be an honest and honorable *hombre*."

"And you?"

He fluttered his hand again. "I have no proof to the contrary."

"But?"

"I've met Sands twice." He rubbed his palm across his midsection. "Instinct, which won't hold up in court, tells me he's somebody I ought not to trust."

"That was my impression, but Kate liked him and trusted him."

"You're no longer married, I hear?"

"Apparently I got a divorce during my stay in the Freezer. She's living down in Mexico now, in Quintana Roo."

"So I heard."

"Have you heard about Dan, about my son?"

"Nothing, no."

"I'd like to see him while I'm across the border. Soon as I run down Dr. Kittridge and—"

A faint hooting sound commenced, and then a panel in the far wall slid open. There was a vidphone alcove behind it.

"That's my tapfree phone. Excuse me." Captain Manzano got up gradually and went over to the phone. "*Sí*?"

Walt Bascom of the Cosmos Detective Agency appeared on the screen, dressed in a different rumpled suit. "Ernie, how are you? Good. You look great. Is Jake there?"

"He is. And I'm glad we've had a chance to have this conversation, Walt."

Taking the captain's place in the alcove, Jake said, "Something important?"

"Dr. Danenberg seems to have resurfaced. She wants to talk to you."

"Where is she? Up in GLA?"

"Down there, specifically in the town of Casas Grandes. That's about one hundred fifty miles south of you, isn't it?"

"About. How do I contact—"

"Tonight at eight she says she'll be in Señor Blue's Café. Can you make that?"

"Sure, but is this going to be the doctor or another sim?"

Bascom shrugged. "Go find out, Jake," he said and hung up.

There was yet another pungent and unpleasant odor in Jake's fifth-floor hotel room when he returned to it late in the afternoon. Halting a few steps beyond the threshold, he dropped his cardkey into his jacket pocket.

Things in the living room appeared to be even more disorderly than when he'd left.

Jake was reaching for the lazgun in his waistband when the door of the bathroom came whipping open.

A large, wide, Mexican cyborg charged out at him. In place of a right hand he had a whirring electric knife.

Feeling somewhat like a matador, Jake pivoted and flattened back against the wall.

The charging cyborg, knifehand buzzing loudly, galloped on by and stopped himself just short of careening out into the corridor through the still open hotel-room doorway.

As the big man started to turn, Jake lunged. He dealt him three sharp blows to the kidneys.

"*Mierda!*" grunted the cyborg, staggering forward, coming close to dropping to his knees.

Jake booted him in the backside.

The cyborg went tumbling into the corridor and landed flat-out on the orange, yellow and red carpeting.

Jake dived toward him.

The man made a growling, muttering noise and lashed out with the blade.

Dodging, Jake kicked out with his booted foot.

The hard toe of the boot struck the cyborg just below the elbow. He cried out in pain and his arm, the knife still flickering at its end, fell limp to his side.

Catching hold of the metal base of the knife, Jake used the man's arm as a lever to snap it away from him. He watched the assailant go staggering away, dancing backward until he slammed into a wall. Then Jake realized the knife and its base had broken completely free of the man's arm.

Blood splashed, along with broken twists of wire and twisted nuts and bolts.

Jake pointed the knife at the man, who was crouched on the floor. "I don't like surprises," he said in Spanish, easing closer. "Now tell me who sent you."

"Screw you," muttered the big man, "and your mother."

"You're going to need a doctor. The sooner you answer my—"

Suddenly the man jerked upward, butting Jake hard in the stomach.

Jake went stumbling back, sideswiping the wall and then dropping to one knee on the worn carpeting of the hallway.

The big man scrambled to his feet, started running. He hit the fifth-floor fire-exit doorway, lopsidedly, with one shoulder. The door bumped open and he headed downstairs.

On one knee Jake was gasping in air. "Let him sucker me," he said, "damn it."

By the time he was upright and able to breathe regularly it was too late to chase the assailant.

Back in his room he checked to make certain no bugs, explosives or other trinkets had been planted. Then he repacked his suitcase, tossing in the knifehand wrapped in a *Paloma Hotel* towel. He phoned the desk and arranged to check out. He left no forwarding address.

It was raining in Casas Grandes. A hard, warm rain that fell straight down through the night. Dodging puddles and potholes, Jake jogged along the curving back street that led to Señor Blue's Café. About a thousand feet up above, a plasbottomed tourist skybus was drifting slowly over.

"Now I'll be part of everybody's vacation memories," reflected Jake, glancing briefly up and getting smacked in the face with the heavy night rain.

Just short of the main entrance to the narrow, neon-trimmed café, he ducked into a thin, quirky alley. At its end was a blue-painted metal door. Turning up his collar again, Jake rapped three longs and two shorts.

"Quién es?" inquired a voxbox.

"It's Jake, P.J."

"Quién?"

"Jake Cardigan, damn it!"

"The voice sounds somewhat like yours."

After another thirty seconds the door opened inward. Jake followed it into a shadowy adobe brick corridor. "Wasn't the secret knock we arranged enough?" he asked.

"I'm being cautious, *Juanito*." At the end of the corridor appeared a small, slim man in a gray suit. "You implied during our recent phone conversation that your rendezvous in my establishment this evening was of an especially secret nature and therefore—"

"Okay, I appreciate the concern, P.J."

P. J. Ramirez was dark, balding and about fifty. He narrowed his left eye, scanning Jake as he approached. "You look very much like my old friend Jake Cardigan."

"So I've been told."

"Con permiso." The small man reached up to tap Jake on the forehead. "No, you don't sound like an android simulacrum." He tapped Jake's skull once again. "You don't have that distinctive android echo."

Grinning, Jake said, "Has Dr. Danenberg arrived, P.J.?"

"But moments ago." He escorted Jake into his office. *"Mira."*

A wall of the office was of seethru one-way plastiglass. It showed the main dining area of the small restaurant.

"I thought you told me business was thriving," mentioned Jake, moving close to the spywall.

"Naturally on a rainy night it slacks off a little, Jake."

There were ten tables and five booths in Señor Blue's Café, plus a small wooden stage. There were seven customers to be seen, and a chrome-plated, guitar-playing robot perched on a stool on the stage.

"What do you think of my new guitar player?"

"Get rid of the sombrero."

"It adds color for the *turistas*."

"At least get rid of the tassels." Sitting alone in the middle booth against the café wall was Dr. Danenberg. Or at least someone who greatly resembled her. "She come in alone?"

"*Sí*, and nobody followed her in here." Ramirez strolled over to his large silver desk. He flipped a switch and a screen mounted on the desk came to life to give a view of the rain-swept street out in front of the place. "There is no one lurking outside either."

Looking from the screen back to Dr. Danenberg, Jake asked, "Anybody inside paying special attention to her?"

"*Nadie*—not a soul."

Jake stood watching. Dr. Danenberg was, carefully, studying the few other patrons of the café. She put her voxwatch to her ear, glanced at the main entryway.

Ramirez asked, "Jake, how was—how was your time in the Freezer?"

"Sorry, P.J., I slept through it. So there's nothing much to tell."

"Be serious. Was it painful, terrifying, anguishing?"

"It wasn't anything." He turned away from the wall, taking a paper-wrapped package from under his jacket. "One further favor." Dropping the package on the silver desk, he unwrapped it. "The gent who used to wear this tried to do me in this afternoon."

Ramirez bent to look at the knifehand, then quickly straightened. "*Dios!* That belongs, I am most nearly certain, to Frankie Torres."

"Who does Torres belong to?"

After backing a few steps farther away from the desk, the café proprietor answered, "Torres is a free-lance, Jake. A very nasty man whom one can hire for odd jobs ranging from debt collecting to murder. He usually hangs out in the Borderland."

"Any idea who might have hired him to slow me down?"

"None," said Ramirez, "but I can—in my usual discreet way—try to find out. This happened in Las Cruces?"

"Just before I took my leave of the Paloma."

"Jake, you oughtn't to stay at places like that. It's beneath you."

"The agency booked it," he said. "Find out, too, how Torres knew I was in town."

"Sí." Ramirez's forehead added wrinkles. "This is a serious business you're involved in."

"I was commencing to suspect that myself. I'll go out and meet the doctor. *Gracias* for your help."

"De nada." He whipped a plyochief out of his trouser pocket. "Before you go meet a lady, wipe that mud off your jacket."

"Can you guarantee that?" Dr. Danenberg was leaning forward on her seat, plump elbows resting on the booth table, stubby fingers intertwined to produce a lump of clutched fists.

"I can't guarantee anything—but I can make arrangements to get you taken safely out of Casas Grandes. After that we just hope."

"Your stay in that penal colony seems to have sapped some of your confidence and . . . why are you staring at me so intently?"

"Could be because I want to make sure I'm not talking to a sim," he said. "Don't let it distract you, doctor."

"I explained why I sent the android dupe, Cardigan." Her fingers unlocked, formed a new pattern. "I was—I still am afraid I'm a target for assassins. Obviously, as was proved at the Boardwalk, my fears are well founded."

"If you'd shared those fears in advance instead of sending a decoy, my partner—"

"I didn't come here to make apologies."

"Okay. Who sent the kamikaze?"

Her stubby fingers parted, she put one hand at each side of the green table. "I suspect several people."

"For instance?"

"Do you know Sonny Hokori?"

"We're old buddies. Do you?"

"Only by reputation. We were aware that he was greatly interested in our researches."

"Anyone else?"

"Several Tek lords, since they all apparently believe I am still actively engaged in anti-Tek research," she said. "And also, though I hesitate to accuse . . ." Her head bowed and the rest of the sentence was lost in a mumble.

"Didn't catch that."

Still not looking up, Dr. Danenberg said, "It's possible that Leon wants me dead."

Jake sat up. "Leon Kittridge?"

She nodded slowly. "For a . . . for a combination of reasons." She raised her head, looking around the café. "Do you think I might have something to drink—a beer perhaps?"

Jake signaled Ramirez, who'd been leaning against the bar, and pantomimed the bringing of two beers. "What would be some of Dr. Kittridge's reasons for wanting you dead?"

"We weren't just colleagues," she said. "There was a time when we were somewhat closer than that." She paused, watching his face. "I know, you assume a man with a daughter as lovely as Beth must have had a lovely wife and would prefer lovely women rather than—"

"Nope, I was wondering why I think you're more attractive than you do."

She said, annoyed, "I'm not in any need of cheap flattery, Cardigan."

Jake waited until Ramirez himself had brought them two bottles of Mexican beer and two chilled glasses, until he'd bowed to the doctor and smiled at Jake and gone politely away. Then he asked, "Kittridge doesn't seem like the kind of guy who resorts to murder to get rid of old loves."

"I wasn't an especially good loser and I gave him a lot of trouble after we parted," she said. "And, too, I know a good deal about his anti-Tek process. He wouldn't want that knowledge to get out, especially if he may intend to sell it."

"Obviously he always meant to sell it—to one government agency or another."

"I mean sell it to someone like Sonny Hokori."

"You have any evidence that Kittridge is planning something like that?"

"No, I have only suspicions."

"What about Bennett Sands—would he be in on anything like that?"

She shook her head. "No, Bennett has always been an honest man—well, as honest as one can be at his level of success. Certainly, though, Bennett would never get involved in any deal with a man like Hokori."

"But he was financing Dr. Kittridge."

"He was a partner, yes, in the development of the new crystal."

"New crystal?"

"I haven't time—nor have you the knowledge probably—to explain the entire process. Suffice it to say that part of Leon's system depends on his discovery of a new synthetic crystal. The crystal is essential in producing the high-frequency oscillation needed to destroy the Tek chips," Danenberg told him a bit impatiently.

"Has he reached the point where he can actually destroy the chips?"

"Leon was nearly there at the time we parted company, Cardigan, and that was some weeks ago. I'm certain that he, especially with Beth helping him, has everything ready for the final testing by now."

"Could that be what he came down here for?"

"I assume so."

"So his notes, his equipment—all that would've been with him in the skycruiser that crashed?"

"If it crashed. It's also possible that it was simply diverted," Dr. Danenberg suggested. "Either with Leon's cooperation or without it."

"And if it was without it, you figure Sonny Hokori might be the one?"

"He or his many competitors."

Jake asked, "You know Kurt Winterguild?"

"Yes, much better actually than I care to."

"He knows what Kittridge is doing?"

"Initially Leon took both Winterguild and his agency into his confidence."

Jake poured his beer into his glass, watching the foam for a few seconds. "You know Beth well, too," he said finally.

"I do."

"If Kittridge is selling out his system to Sonny Hokori or any of the Tek kingpins, would she be likely to go along?"

The doctor took a long swallow of her beer, directly from the bottle. "Do you know her yourself?"

"Not actually, no."

"But you've—of course, as an operative for the Cosmos Detective Agency, you would have—you've seen her picture and possibly vidfootage." She drank again. "Many men tend to become quite taken with her and, possibly to their misfortune, they idealize Beth some."

"That could be, but do you think she'd be in cahoots with her father in anything illegal?"

"I'd say it was possible." She finished her beer. "If you'd be so kind as to order me another. I have something else to mention to you."

Jake signaled Ramirez again, holding up one finger. "About Beth?"

Her laugh was thin and nasal. "No, about them both, actually," she said. "Decades ago a great many American and European companies—especially those in electronics—had modest-sized assembly plants all over Mexico. The wages here are—"

"They call them *maquiladoras*."

"Yes, exactly, Cardigan, and the Tek runners have taken over many of them to produce Tek chips and assemble Brainboxes." She smiled as Ramirez set down her second beer. "Something like two years ago Leon bought himself one of those *maquiladoras* in this area, not more than fifty miles to the west of us here. He turned it into a field laboratory and, I believe—though I haven't visited it in over a year—that he was doing some anti-Tek work there as well."

"Be a good place to visit then. Can you guide me to—"

"No, but I've drawn you a map." She reached into a side pocket of her jacket, producing a folded sheet of tan paper and an electrokey. "You won't have any trouble finding it—and you may indeed learn something of value, Cardigan." She dropped the map and the key next to his glass.

The aircar, rented from a cousin of P. J. Ramirez, started to sputter. Jake was, according to the instruments that were still working on the control panel, approximately twenty miles from his destination and two thousand feet from the ground.

The rain was hitting at the windshield and the whole cabin was echoing from the drumming of the raindrops. Down below him, from what Jake could make out through the nightvision, seethru bottom of the cabin, there was nothing but dark, thick jungle.

The sputtering accelerated to a loud series of stuttering pops.

Jake leaned, scanned the panel and located the Status button. He jabbed it with his forefinger.

The voxbox blurted something in slurred Spanish.

Jake didn't catch it. "*Otra vez,*" he requested.

"The engine," said the Status voxbox in English this time, "having reached the guaranteed two hundred thousand airmiles, is about to give up the ghost."

"Install a replacement," he instructed the car.

"In this model aircar, that has to be done manually by the driver or a qualified mechanic."

"Where are the spare engines housed?"

"There is an emergency engine, good for at least ten thousand airmiles, stored in the handy compartment beneath the driveseat."

After punching out an automatic flight pattern, Jake got himself free of the seat and slid open the drawer beneath it. There was nothing in there but a picnic hamper.

He pried it open and found only the remains of a picnic lunch from some months ago.

"Where do we store the food?"

"Compartment to your rear, opening now."

That was where the engine had been stored. It was a compact one, about the size of a brick. Jake carried it, listening uneasily to the explosive popping of the current engine, over to the floor compartment marked MOTOR.

He opened the lid, studied the dying engine for a few seconds and then, gingerly, removed it.

The aircar fell silent.

He connected the emergency engine.

The aircar remained silent.

Jake gave the newly installed device a moderate punch with the left fist.

It took hold and started working; the aircar bounced twice in the rain-swept air.

Back in the driveseat, he took over the control of the craft.

He looked below him again and saw the factory that Dr. Kittridge had converted to a laboratory. It was coming up directly below.

There were no lights showing, no sign that anyone was in or around the place.

Jake flew on to a small clearing about a quarter of a mile beyond and punched out a landing pattern.

The descent was relatively smooth, although a few treetops got clipped. The landing was only minimally jarring.

Jake sat there for a moment. "Nothing as comforting as rain on a metal roof." He got out of the driveseat and went to the door.

He took his handlight out of his trouser pocket, opened the door and stood listening. He heard nothing but rain, rain hitting the treetops, rain hitting the tree trunks, rain hitting the brush, rain hitting the muddy ground circling his landed car.

He decided, after a bit more than three minutes, that there was no one around and that his advent had gone unnoticed.

Taking a deep breath, Jake clicked on his light and looked down. "That's mud all right," he observed and dropped clear of the cabin.

He stayed crouched in the brush some hundred yards from the *maquiladora* for five minutes after he located the place. He was already pretty well soaked, so the extra five minutes didn't appreciably add to his dampness.

The factory consisted of three long, low, metal and plastiglass buildings linked together and looking like a row of greenhouses. There was not a single light showing. In the soggy minutes of his vigil Jake hadn't spotted or sensed the presence of anyone at all in the vicinity.

"So this is probably not an ambush arranged for me by Dr. Danenberg." Standing, he took a final look around and then went running across the mud and gravel that surrounded the old factory site.

The electrokey that the doctor had provided him worked on the rear door of the nearest glass and metal building.

The door whirred, clicked and swung open inward.

Jake hesitated on the threshold.

A smell that mixed damp ground, burned plas and some chemicals he couldn't identify came pouring out at him.

He waited another minute, then stepped into the darkness.

Nothing happened.

Carefully and quietly Jake shut the door behind him. The darkness swallowed him up.

He stayed still, slightly hunched, for another minute before turning on his light.

This big room of the old factory had never been remodeled or refurbished. It was filled with dusty workbenches and a few rusty, defunct workbots. Several plaswood cartons were stacked in a corner, festooned with cobwebs and splotched with black mildew.

Jake walked on into the second room of the *maquiladora.* This had been partly converted and subdivided into living quarters. The floors, though, weren't completed and had gaps in the planking.

Several partitions were in place, but no new room had been completed.

The kitchen unit was the most nearly finished and the larder was stocked with freezedry and dehyde meals. There was a round metal table with three chairs. At one of the places sat a plasmug with a thick coating of greenish scum floating atop of whatever liquid it contained.

The night rain was coming down enthusiastically, pelting the walls and roof of the long building.

Leaving the kitchen, Jake moved on to enter the third and final building. The door was locked and he had to use the electrokey again.

The door opened inward and he followed it into the final room.

The door shut quietly behind him and soft white light blossomed all around him. The plastiglass walls had been blacked out and the whole large, long room had been converted into a thoroughly equipped electronics lab.

But what Jake paid attention to was the spotless white table at the exact center of the white room. Lying faceup on the table was the naked body of a young woman.

It was Beth Kittridge.

But it wasn't Beth Kittridge.

Jake knew that when he was still ten feet away from the softly glowing white table.

"Thank God," he said. He didn't want to find her dead.

What was lying on the table was an impressively realistic android simulacrum of Beth Kittridge. The mechanical replica of the missing young woman was not quite finished.

Jake noticed now the small rectangular gap beneath her left breast. Some inner circuitry showed, plus a few dangling and unconnected strands of varicolored wire.

He stopped beside the table, staring down at the android. Beth was very pretty and she looked so lost and vulnerable lying there in the white light.

Jake glanced around, seeking something to cover her with. "Hey," he reminded himself, "it's only an andy."

He was feeling even more strongly that he had met Beth somewhere before. And that in the long, enforced sleep up in the Freezer she was one of the people he'd dreamed about.

Frowning, shivering slightly in his wet clothes, Jake slowly circled the body. High above, the rain drummed on the lab roof.

"This is a hell of a sophisticated mechanism," he said. "As good as if not better than the one Dr. Danenberg sent to meet me and Gomez at the Boardwalk."

Beth's father must have intended this to serve as a stand-in for his daughter. Sure, he knew there was trouble coming from the Tek overlords and he wanted to have a decoy—wanted to protect her from the kind of danger that almost hit Dr. Danenberg. But for some reason they'd had to take off before the android was finished.

Jake halted near the skull of the simulacrum, leaned down and studied the young woman's face. "They must've downloaded a dupe of the contents of Beth's mind into the brain of this thing," he reflected. "Had to, otherwise it could never do any kind of adequate job impersonating her."

So it was likely this replica knew just about everything the actual Beth knew. At least up to the time she and her father had left here.

"Damn—if I could just get her to talk to me . . ."

And why couldn't he?

The sim looked to be nearly completed, only a few final hookups were needed. The job shouldn't take more than a couple hours at most.

Jake knew something about electronics and robotics. Obviously he could never himself build anything this complex, but he just might be able to get this one working. Get it functioning at least well enough to tell him something.

"I'm not all that anxious to sit around chatting with an android," he said, moving back from the body. "But I definitely need more information about the Kittridges, and this gadget should be a good source."

He prowled the laboratory and in less than fifteen minutes he'd gathered together enough tools and gear for his attempt to bring the replica of Beth to life.

"No, that doesn't feel quite exactly right."

Straightening, Jake took a quick step back from the lab table. He was staring at the android, who'd just spoken.

The sound of the heavy night rain seemed all at once to fade away.

Beth sat up on the table, touching at the gap beneath her breast. "You've done just about everything okay up to now," she said, smiling approvingly at him. "Which is why I'm functioning. But you've put the wrong— Here, it's easier if I just show you." Deftly she inserted both her thumbs and forefingers into the hole in her chest. "You, see—have to hook this red wire to the green one. You've got it connected to the blue one, which is not going to work too well." Smiling more broadly, she took a look around the lab. "The piece you need to close up this rent in my chest is sitting on that counter yonder."

"Maybe you'd like to have some clothes, too." Jake could hear the rain again.

The pretty, dark-haired young woman swung gracefully off the table, walked across to the counter and picked up her missing part. "Your reactions are interesting, you know," she said as she fitted the fleshtone section in place and tapped at it. "Does that look all right?"

"A perfect fit."

"What I'm getting at is—when I was dormant, you probably thought of me as just a machine. But now that I'm—well, let's call it alive—now you're embarrassed."

"Not exactly. I thought you might be cold."

She brushed a strand of long dark hair back from her forehead. "No, actually when I'm too cold to function properly, a signal goes off inside my skull. One, of course, only I can hear." She turned to him and held out her right hand. "I'm Beth Kittridge—well, you know what I mean. An android simulacrum of Beth, containing all her memories, feelings and so on."

"I'm Jake Cardigan." He hesitated before going ahead and shaking hands. Her flesh felt real and warm.

"You're a human, not an android. I can tell," she said.

"How?"

She shrugged her naked shoulders. "I'm not exactly certain, Mr. Cardigan. It's just another of my built-in instincts. My father and Dr. Danenberg both design androids that are considerably more talented than anything else on the market today. But that sounds like I'm trying to sell you one, doesn't it?" Laughing, she walked over to a wall cabinet. "Now I'll get myself dressed—so you'll feel more at ease." Opening the cabinet, she started looking over the clothes that were shelved there. "Father spoke highly of you, by the way, which is why I won't bother to use this on you." She momentarily pointed the stunpistol she'd grabbed off a shelf in his direction. "Your record as a cop wasn't all that admirable toward the end, but we concluded you'd been framed."

"I didn't realize that you and your father—that Beth and her father were aware of me," Jake told her. "Had we met someplace or other?"

She studied him for several silent seconds before shaking her head. "No, I don't believe so. But father and I are interested in the Tek trade and the lawmen involved in combating it. And, after all, you were a well-known police officer in your day."

"In my day."

"Well, it was—what? Five years ago at least that they sent you up to the Freezer." She placed the gun on a counter and started getting into a pair of neodenim trousers.

"Only four years actually."

"That probably seems a longer time to me than it does to someone your age." Beth was pulling a sweatertunic on over her head.

"Hey, I'm not even fifty yet."

After she finished dressing, Beth slipped the gun into a belt holster. "Maybe now you can explain why you're here, Mr. Cardigan," she suggested, facing him. "As well as why you activated me."

Jake studied her and then grinned slowly. "How much like the actual Beth Kittridge are you?"

"Exactly like her, since Father built me to be a dead ringer," she answered. "But then they had to rush off to visit Bennett Sands before he had a chance to complete me quite." She paused, frowning at him. "Has something happened to them? Is that why you're here?"

"We'd better talk about it."

Beth was sitting on the edge of the lab table with her long legs dangling down, watching Jake as he paced. Outside in the night thunder rumbled in the jungle. "Then they both might be dead?" she was asking.

"I don't know. That's what I came down here across the border to find out. Tell me where they were heading when they left here."

The dark-haired android rubbed a hand along her thigh. "Keep in mind, Mr. Cardigan, that my memories stop several days ago," she said. "At that time my father and I—and Beth, rather—were planning to visit Bennett Sands shortly at the home he has in the state of Chihuahua."

"You mentioned earlier that an emergency had come up, causing them to leave ahead of schedule."

"That was only an assumption. Since my father had been intending to take me and not Beth on the trip—well, something urgent must've occurred or else I'd have gone and Beth would be safely hiding out somewhere."

"The emergency had something to do with Sands?"

She shrugged, spreading her hands wide. "I'm guessing it did, judging from where they were when the skycruiser went down."

"How exactly is Sands involved in all this business?"

"He was financing my father in his development of his anti-Tek system." A frown touched her forehead; she rubbed at her leg again. "I've never been as fond of Bennett as my father is."

"Don't trust him?"

"Well, he always manages to sound very upright and dedicated, eager to develop an anti-Tek system for the good of humanity and all that crap." Beth shook her head slowly. "Very altruistic, you know, and swearing he's only interested in minimum profits."

"But you think he was out for something more?"

"It's only a feeling. Although . . ."

"Although what?"

"The past few weeks my father has been getting increasingly—well, evasive. I suspect, really, that he's been having communications with Bennett that he hasn't told me about."

"That's unusual?"

"Oh, yes, we always discuss everything openly," Beth told him. "No secrets—or very few—between us."

"You've worked closely with him on this anti-Tek system, haven't you?"

"Yes, certainly."

"Then you know all about the synthetic crystal and the specific oscillation required to destroy—"

"I know all about it. But how come you do, Mr. Cardigan?"

"Dr. Danenberg told me quite a—"

"Oh, yes. Poor Hilda."

"Why did she and your father quit working together?"

She leaned forward. "What is it you're actually after?"

"I told you—my detective agency has been hired to find out what happened to Dr. Kittridge and Beth. Our client is the Moonbase-Hartford insurance outfit."

"Then it doesn't seem my father's anti-Tek system should be of any interest to you at all."

"It is, though, since it could be the reason he and Beth disappeared. Plus which, I'd like to see it put to use eventually."

"Okay, then there's one more reason why I'm valuable to you. I can duplicate just about everything my father's done thus far."

He nodded. "Exactly why I want to get you to a safe place as soon as I can. After that, I'll head for—"

"I intend to go with you—to help find my father."

Jake quit pacing and shook his head. "I'm working on this one alone," he told her firmly.

"But it makes more sense," she insisted, "if we work together."

"Nope. We'll exchange information here and now, then I'll see that you get safely stored someplace."

"Is it because you don't want to work with an android?"

"I'm not especially anxious to work with anyone."

"But you started off with a partner—Gomez, you said his name was."

"He's in the hospital. So for now I—"

"I know the route my father probably took. I know Mexico."

"So do I."

"Yes, but I also know Beth."

"Even so. You're not going to tag—"

Up above them near the shadowy ceiling a bank of five red bulbs of light suddenly started flashing urgently.

Smiling at him, Beth dropped free of the table. "It looks like we're going to be forced to team up."

"What is it?"

"Trouble." She went running to the door of another cabinet, pulling it open wide. She reached inside and brought out two powerful stunrifles. "Father prefers to stun intruders." She came striding back toward him and tossed him one of the rifles.

Jake caught it and nodded up at the flashing lights. "That's a warning of intruders?"

"Yes. Someone's already inside the first building and coming our way." She glanced toward the door Jake had used earlier. "We don't have as effective a security system as we ought."

An enormous rumble of thunder sounded outside; the walls of the old factory rattled. At that same moment the metal entry door began to glow a harsh, shimmering blue. In just a few seconds it ceased to be, turning to a flickering, glowing grit that collapsed to the floor.

Three large, rain-soaked men were framed in the doorway. They wore water-spattered plas ponchos, and their wet hair was plastered to their skulls.

The largest of the three was Frankie Torres, the cyborg who'd tried to kill Jake back at his hotel. He had a new hand screwed into the socket of his right arm, this one a blunt-nosed lazgun.

"*Cabrón!*" he shouted when he recognized Jake. Shedding water, making a blubbering, snarling noise, he broke free of the other two and came charging into the lab.

Jake had dropped to the floor some seconds earlier, gone rolling over the floor until he hit a wall, and then come up with his stunrifle aimed directly at the onrushing Torres.

Torres' gunhand had been swinging wildly, trying to stay focused on the fast-moving Jake.

Beth had scurried to the lab table, swung it around and planted it between herself and the armed intruders.

The other two came in as a pair, then split and dived in opposite directions. Each held a long-barreled lazgun. Each fired into the laboratory. Their shots went wild.

Jake's first bolt of fierce scarlet light out of his stunrifle missed Torres by a good six inches.

Torres fired and missed, too. The blast sliced a chunk out of a counter roughly three feet above Jake.

"My turn." Beth popped to her feet and fired her stunrifle at Torres. She dropped back down behind the table.

Her sizzling scarlet stunbeam took the cyborg in the side.

He made a gagging noise and his head started to tick back and forth, as though there were something caught in his throat that he was struggling to get rid of. He lurched sideways, striving to raise his gunhand and get it aimed once again at Jake. But the gun seemed to weigh an enormous amount now, seemed to be pulling him downward.

Torres followed the gun toward the floor. It went off, cutting a wobbly circle in the tiles. Dust and jagged chips of plas came swirling up in a cloud. The cyborg fell into that and hit with a great thud. He twitched violently from head to foot, sighing out a long, sad breath. After that he lay stiff and still.

Jake meantime had moved again. And, as he scattered, he fired at one of the other invaders.

The man, who had a mustache that looked too big for his lean face, fired his lazgun at Jake simultaneously.

He missed, but Jake didn't.

The man's arms went up and he started to flap them in a limp, disjointed way, like someone who felt compelled to complete some strange exercise.

While the second man was dropping down into unconsciousness, the third fired at Beth.

His shot sliced the lab table nearly in half.

But Beth was no longer behind it. She was running, in a low crouch, toward the opposite wall. Halting, she dropped to one knee, aimed the rifle and fired.

The beam hit him in the exact middle of his body. Beads of water flew from his poncho and it billowed up around him. He dropped straight to the floor, sat wide-legged. The poncho settled around his body and masked his last convulsive spasms before he passed out.

"Not bad," said Jake to the young woman, getting to his feet.

Brushing back her hair, she stood up. Then she glanced up at the warning lights. "They're flashing again. That means more visitors. We'd best get out of here."

"Agreed."

She hurried over to him and led him to the opposite wall. "There's a concealed escape door. Let's hope I really am an exact replica." Shifting her rifle, she pressed her right palm to the recog panel.

It pinged; the door slid open. A corridor was revealed. They started along it and the door shut swiftly at their backs.

"There's a spare skycar in the storeroom this passway'll lead us to," she explained as they ran along side by side. "We can use it to get clear of here."

"Since we don't know how many more of them there are, retreating is probably the best idea."

Beth said, "I think this means, Mr. Cardigan, that we're going to be partners—at least for a while."

"Apparently so," he admitted. "And you might as well call me Jake."

The doors of the hidden shed whipped automatically open. Beth guided the skycar out into the rainy night, taxied across a stretch of clearing and sent the craft climbing into the surrounding darkness.

Glancing over at Jake, she smiled. "You're not used to riding in the passenger seat."

"I'd feel more comfortable at the controls."

"Then our partnership's going to be an especially valuable experience for you, something that'll expand your range of experience and build your character," she informed him. "That's how my father likes to describe anything that I initially turn my nose up at."

"Yeah, my father handed out similar slogans." Jake slouched in his seat. "Most of them, though, didn't turn out to be true."

"Is he still alive?"

"Nope."

"You didn't like him."

"It was, actually, the other way around."

"That's too bad," Beth said as the skycar rose above the trees and leveled off. "What's our destination, by the way?"

"Right now just head in the general direction of the state of Chihuahua."

The dark-haired young woman punched out a flight pattern on the control panel. "What was your father?"

"Military man—professional soldier."

"Stationed where?"

"Mexico, Central America, Brazil."

"So that's how you got to know this country, traveling with him?"

"He usually didn't take us with him, my mother and I. But after she died, he allowed me, reluctantly, to live with him here in Mexico."

"My father and I . . . Damn!" She was frowning at the dash panel. A tiny rectangular screen there had come flashing to life; a bulb of red light beneath it was flashing. "We're being chased."

Jake saw a picture of a heavy black skycruiser on the little screen. It was coming up fast on their tail from the jungle below. "Let me take the controls."

Beth shook her head, her long hair brushing at her shoulders. "I can outfly most anybody, Jake," she assured him. "My father taught me originally, and there was also a professional skyracer I used to be fond of."

"How well armed are we?"

"Just a disabler beam in the tail."

"Nothing lethal?"

"My father doesn't believe in that."

"Okay, I'll handle the tail-gunner job." Unbuckling, he left his seat and double-timed flat-footed to the gunner chair at the rear of their skycar.

He could see the big cruiser climbing closer through the heavy rain.

"Hang on," advised Beth.

She gunned the skycar and it shot ahead, climbed and then started to execute a zigzagging backward loop.

Jake found himself hanging upside down in the gunner seat.

They started to pass upside down over the pursuing skycruiser.

The bigger craft had a lazcanon mounted on each of its stubby wings. Two thick, crackling lines of purplish light came knifing through the night rain. They converged on the spot where the skycar would have been if Beth hadn't gone into the loop.

Jake thumbed the trigger button of the disabler gun.

"C'mon, Jake," urged the young woman, "you can do better than that."

His first try had missed the pursuing craft entirely.

"Okay," he said through clenched teeth and fired again.

The next intense burst of green light touched the tail of the black cruiser. All at once the whole craft glowed a sputtering green. It swayed from side to side in the rain-swept sky, its engine put out of action by the beam of the disabler. It dropped down in bouncing jerks, nosed over, dived toward the dark jungle below.

The skycruiser flirted with the dark treetops for a while, almost hitting them and then pulling up free in time to miss. Finally it had to give up and went into a sharp downward plunge.

"Not too bad." Beth brought their skycar around and into an upright position again. "I suppose you're rusty—which is only to be expected."

"I hit the damn thing."

She held up two fingers on her left hand. "Second try."

He saw the skycruiser crash to a rough landing in the woodlands. Nodding, he left the gunner perch and came back to sit next to Beth. "How about a truce between you and me?"

She let her eyes go wide for a second. "Oh, don't you and your other partners kid each other good-naturedly now and then?"

"Good-naturedly."

She smiled at him, then tapped the dash panel. "Nobody else on our tail," she announced, pleased.

"You fly pretty well."

"Yes, I do."

"I'm wondering how those goons knew we were here."

"Mightn't they have followed you?"

"No, nobody tagged me out of Casas Grandes."

"Dr. Danenberg perhaps told someone."

"I saw her to a safe hideaway before heading for here," he said. "Who else knows about the lab?"

"A few others."

"Including Bennett Sands?"

"He's familiar with it, of course. He's even visited us there," she said. "You don't trust him either, do you?"

"Not especially."

For nearly five seconds after he awakened, Jake had no idea where he was. Sitting up, he mumbled a few words.

A new day was starting, the sky outside their droning skycar was a thin, pale blue.

"We're almost there," Beth told him, punching out a landing pattern on the dash.

"That's the town of Cuidado down there?"

"It is, yes."

The skycar started dropping down through the morning. Directly below was a large, domed structure with TORO PLAZA inscribed atop it in huge gloletters.

"I seem to have dozed off."

"You were tired. A man of your age can't, after all, expect to tangle with a band of louts and not feel weary afterward."

"Wait now." He turned, studying her profile while rubbing at a spot on the back of his neck. "I recollect that you reached over and touched me, right after we got through discussing our destination. Yeah, and I felt a faint tingling and . . . I fell asleep."

She said, "It's just one of the built-in knacks I have."

"You stunned me?"

"Nothing so drastic, no." She glanced at him, smiling carefully. "You looked as though you needed some sleep, but were—"

"Don't," suggested Jake, taking hold of her arm, "do anything like that again, Beth. For as long as we're forced to be together, you let me make the decisions."

"It's not all that important, Jake. I simply—"

"It is, though. I don't want you using any of your gadgetry on me."

"All right, okay. I'm sorry."

"How many other tricks like that can you do?"

"I have," she admitted, "a few other knacks. My father decided he might as well build the best simulacrum possible. One that was better than a human in some ways."

"That's fine." Jake concentrated on looking down at Cuidado, which was a medium-sized city along the border that separated the states of Sonora and Chihuahua.

"Truly, I won't do anything like that again."

"I'm just not fond of having anyone put me to sleep."

"Yes, I should've realized."

The skycar circled a public landing area, then settled down to a landing. Yellow dust came swirling up as the craft touched ground.

Activating the door release, Beth said, "Don't sulk. Okay?"

"I'm not sulking." He got free of his seat, dropped down to the yellow ground.

"What would you do if Gomez did something you didn't like," she asked, joining him, "to clear the air?"

"Punch him."

"Oh," she said, laughing. "Well, you probably can't do that to me—at least not here in public. Would you like to stop for breakfast?"

They were walking along a narrow street, and most of the small shops and restaurants were starting to open for the day. Already the scents of coffee and spices were in the air.

"Might as well," said Jake. "Then we'll see about our hotel rooms."

"The Flauta Restaurant up ahead has a good rating in Shedenhelm's Travel Guide," she said, nodding at the sidewalk café coming up on their right. "Three stars."

"You've been here before?"

"No, but I have several guidebooks in my memory banks."

Allowing himself to grin, Jake took her arm and guided her to a table. "Do you . . . Shall I order you breakfast?"

Beth smiled. "I don't require food, if that's what you're asking," she said, sitting opposite him. "But I can take in food if necessary to back up the illusion that I'm human. Right now I'll just have a cup of coffee, for appearances' sake."

There were exactly a dozen small, round, white tables arranged on the red-tile paving in front of the Flauta. Only three of the others were occupied so far, each by a tourist couple.

A menu appeared on the small screen at Jake's place. "Language, *por favor*?" inquired an unseen voxbox.

"Make it English," replied Jake.

The original menu vanished, replaced by one in English. "You may give your orders directly to me," instructed the voxbox.

"*Gracias.*"

"*De nada*."

Beth rested an elbow on the table. "We can make do with one room, by the way, Jake. Since I don't require sleep, it—"

"Two."

"It's not a question of propriety, is it?"

"Nope, it's a question of my liking to be by myself now and then."

"All right. I suppose it will look better, too," she said. "What about your contact here in Cuidado? Will he get in touch with you or—"

"We'll have to do some scouting around. The main thing is not to attract too much attention while we're here."

"I can see—"

"It is! It's Jake Cardigan, none other." A tall, lean black man of about thirty-five was hurrying over to their table, smiling broadly. "And—my God! It's Beth Kittridge. Jake, old man, you've found the missing Kittridge girl. Damn—what a news story this is going to make!"

The black man seated himself, uninvited, at the third chair at their table. Smiling, first at Beth, then at Jake, he removed a small recorder-mike from the inner breast pocket of his pale yellow jacket. Placing it in the exact middle of the tabletop, he activated it and said, "We've met before, Miss Kittridge. That was, if you don't quite recall, when I interviewed your father two years ago at a reception at SoCal Tech. I'm Ogden Swires, with *GLA Week*, the leading faxzine on the West Coast. I'd—"

"Before we start the interview," suggested Jake, reaching over to click off the recorder, "how about a little polite social discourse, Og?"

"Jake, hey, you're interfering with my pursuit of a big story."

"For instance, what the hell are you doing in Cuidado? It's not part of Greater Los Angeles."

The reporter moved his hand toward his recorder-mike, noticed Jake's face and withdrew it. "I came down to do a story on Warbride, since our readers are avidly interested in what goes on across the border," he replied. "I've been sitting on my toke for three days, old man, waiting for one of her public relations people to get back to me."

"Public relations?" Jake laughed. "Sounds like she's upgraded her operations quite a lot."

Turning, slowly, to Beth, Swires inquired, "Is your father alive?"

Beth answered, "I haven't as yet agreed to an interview, Mr. Swires."

"*GLA Week* has a guaranteed circulation of four million, Miss Kittridge. You really shouldn't ignore that sort of coverage or—"

"Were you hunting for us?" Jake asked him. "Is that how our paths happened to cross this morning?"

The reporter shook his head. "Old man, I had no idea you were in Mexico at all, nor was I aware that Miss Kittridge had been located." He started to inch his left hand toward the small recorder. "But, as you well know, I really do seem to have a knack for nosing out news."

"That's interesting." Jake grinned at him. "Miss Kittridge and I were just now discussing her knacks."

"Listen, Jake, there are at least a dozen other newspeople in town, trying to insinuate themselves across the border into Chihuahua one way or another," Swires told him. "Amongst them, old man, are a couple from GLA who aren't anywhere near as sympathetic toward you as I am. You remember how I covered your trial, don't you? I was on your side."

" 'Jake Cardigan isn't as big a scoundrel as he's being painted,' was one of your lines that's stuck in my mind."

"Christ, I was practically doing PR for you," insisted Swires. "That wasn't easy, believe me, considering who owns *GLA Week* and who they're friendly with."

Jake caught his arm. "What do you mean? I thought the Reisberson family controlled your faxzine."

Swires nodded and pulled, cautiously, free. "They do, but they're especially close to Bennett Sands—who also does a great deal of advertising with us."

"And?"

"He put a lot of pressure on them back then, Jake. He charged that I was being much too favorable to you, insisted he was dead certain you were deeply involved in Tek running."

"I didn't know that. You should've told me."

"Hell, by the time I found out for certain you were . . ." He glanced toward Beth, then up into the brightening morning sky. "You were unreachable."

"I know where Jake's been." Beth brushed at her dark hair with her right hand.

"I wasn't sure." He smiled at her. "I'm a very polite and discreet interviewer, never going into offensive or unsettling topics. At least, I can be in cases such as yours, Miss Kittridge. May I ask you a few simple questions now?"

Beth rested a hand on his shoulder. "I don't see why not," she said. "Since you're a good friend of Jake's, you're probably the most logical reporter for me to . . . Mr. Swires, is something wrong?"

Approximately three seconds after she'd touched him, the reporter slumped in his chair. Then, starting to snore politely, he went tipping forward until his head was resting on the table.

Jake nodded at the plump couple at the nearest occupied table, who had interrupted their breakfast to stare. "We warned him about drinking so early in the day," he said.

Beth stood. "We'd better just leave him to sleep it off."

"Yes, that's an excellent idea." Jake got up, too.

"Are you ready to order?" asked the voxbox.

"Plenty of black coffee for our friend," said Beth, taking hold of Jake's hand.

Tucking her legs under her, Beth settled into the vinyl armchair near Jake's bed. "I don't think that's what you feel at all," she was saying.

They had ground-floor rooms in the small town-edge inn Jake had decided to come to. Out beyond his one-way plasglass sliding doors was a patio that was nearly overgrown with bright flowering bushes.

Jake was pacing from the open doorway of Beth's adjoining room to the sliding doors. "Nearly noon," he remarked, halting to gaze out into the sunbright patio.

"We're not discussing your contact or why he's late getting back to you," she reminded. "I was asking why you get so damn uneasy whenever I mention your wife or Bennett Sands."

"I'm not clear what you're getting at, Beth. And since it doesn't seem to have anything to do with—"

"Sure, it does. You just found out that Sands took an active part in getting you convicted."

"Nope, all I found out is that Swires was trying to con me into letting him interview you."

"He wasn't lying."

"Do you have a built-in gadget to detect lying, too?"

"It's only an assumption."

"I've spent most of my life questioning people." Turning his back to the sunlight, he frowned down at her.

"Well, then, you ought to be able to tell he wasn't making up a story to put you in a good mood."

"Okay, let's suppose Sands did want to get me sent up to the Freezer. What has that got to do with Kate?"

"You're the one who seems to think it has something to do with her."

"She was working for Sands at the time. That's all."

"And you've been wondering why she never told you what he was up to."

"Sands may not have been up to anything."

"You trusted her."

"Of course, sure." Jake went to the bed and sat on its edge. "There's no need to talk about this any further."

"Didn't you and Gomez talk about it at the time?"

"Not much, no."

"What did he think of Kate?"

"His opinions don't match mine, but we've never much agreed about women. Or clothes. You ought to see some of the—"

"All I'm trying to get at is this," she cut in. "It may turn out that Kate is involved with what's going on right now. If you're still feeling sentimental about her, that could screw us up. I want to find my father and we can't afford to—"

"He's not your father, he's Beth's father." He was on his feet, jabbing a forefinger in the air. "You're nothing more than a goddamn machine. Quit, just quit trying to tell me that my wife was sleeping with Sands or that she helped set me up."

Slowly she stood. "I wasn't going to be that direct about it." Beth moved to the doorway that linked their rooms. She went into hers, but left the door open.

The call didn't come until nearly dusk.

Jake was pacing again when the vidphone in the narrow alcove across from his bed buzzed. Dropping into the plazchair, he flipped the respond switch. "Yeah?"

A fat, smiling man in a pale blue suit appeared on the small image screen. "*Perdóname* for taking so long, Jake," he began, pausing to wipe at his perspiring forehead with a cloth handkerchief. "These are complex and troubled times, and to arrange even the simplest of meetings requires—"

"Have you set up a meeting, Globo?"

"*Sí,* of course. My skills have, if anything, ripened since last we met, Señor Jake."

"Who do I see?"

Globo wiped his forehead again, glancing offscreen. "He calls himself Sombra."

"C'mon—the Shadow?"

"Many of these revolutionists have a melodramatic streak," explained Jake's local contact man. "It would be best not to chide this one about his romantic illusions."

"Don't intend to," he assured the fat man. "How close to Warbride is he?"

"Sombra has arranged several previous meetings with her. He's the only trustworthy liaison in Cuidado," answered Globo. "He's the one who set up the *Time/Life* faxzine interview two months ago."

"Missed that one. Where and when do I talk to the guy?"

"*Siete,* seven tonight. Do you know how to get to the Toro Plaza?"

"Sure, saw it coming in."

"You meet him in the Matador Pavilion."

"Why get together where there are going to be people around to—"

"The Plaza, since it featured only robot bulls and matadors, did not thrive," explained his informant. "It has been defunct and deserted since last May. Tonight you'll find Gate B unlocked."

"Okay, thanks for arranging this."

"You pay my fee, I do my job. All routine, Jake," said the sweating fat man. "One other thing—Sombra specifies that you meet him entirely alone."

"I wasn't planning to guide a gaggle of *turistas* there."

"It's your reporter friends he's concerned about."

"I don't have any reporter friends."

"And police friends?"

"None hereabouts."

"Then all is *muy bien,* is it not? *Adiós.*" The screen went blank.

"This doesn't sound quite right," commented Beth from the connecting doorway.

"Why?"

"Meeting place is too isolated."

"I've had lots of meetings in isolated spots over the years." He left the chair. "Don't fret while I'm away."

"You're going alone?"

"As specified," he replied. "Fact is, I'd better leave right about now. I want to get there in time to look around some."

She came into the room. "Be careful."

"Always am," he said, clearing his throat. "Beth, I think I'd better apologize for . . . for what I said to you this afternoon."

"For calling me an android? That's okay, I am an android," she said. "It's probably a good idea to remind me of that every so often, so I don't get delusions of humanity."

"The problem is—well, there are still some things I'm not exactly ready to talk about."

"Yes, I understand." She moved in front of him, then leaned up and kissed him on the cheek, putting both arms around him. "Good luck."

He moved back from her after a few seconds, saying, "Thanks."

She smiled, asking, "First time you've been kissed by a machine?"

"I guess it is," he admitted, turning away.

The big tourist landbus rolled smoothly and comfortably through the bright, glowing center of the town's nightlife section. The thousands of lights glaring and flashing outside turned the off-white interior of the bus into a multicolored quilt.

Jake was sitting alone in a seat near the front of the only partially filled vehicle. He was confident he looked enough like a tourist to get fairly close to the Toro Plaza unnoticed.

Two seats ahead of him a thin redheaded young man was aiming his handheld botcamera out the window. "Terrific, terrific," he observed, chuckling. "The contrast will make a nifty social com—"

"Why in the heck do you want another picture of a raggedy man with no legs?" asked the thin blonde young woman beside him.

"You don't get the point, Marcella."

"I guess I sure don't, Rudy."

"See, that guy out there happens to be a vet. You can tell by his tattered Mexican Army uniform," explained Rudy. "Most likely he was disabled during the recent fighting over in Chihuahua. Now we find him begging in the midst of all this glitter, and that makes a nifty social com—"

"He could have legs if he wanted to," the young woman pointed out. "I heard on the vidnews in the hotel room just yesterday that they do that for every veteran. If you lose a limb in the service of your country, they—"

"Maybe the poor bastard's making his own kind of social comment. By refusing to let—"

"Showing off, wallowing in self-pity. And if you think for a minute, Rudy, that when we get back home to Binghamton you're going to inflict endless pictures of raggedy bums on our friends, you are sadly—"

"Shut up, Marcella, and let me shoot this before we pass out of range."

"The lady's right, sir," said the voxbox of the camera. "You've taken more than enough disgusting photographs since arriving in Cuidado. How about instead snapping that jolly street musician coming up—the roly-poly guitar player with the tassels on his sombrero?"

"Shit," commented Rudy, dropping the camera to his lap.

"We'll be halting for a leg-stretch and a snack at the next corner, folks," announced the robot driver. He was big and chrome-plated, wearing a sombrero.

Jake was scanning the bright-lit twilight street. The town had changed quite a lot since he'd been here three—make it seven—years ago. Looming up large on the right was a multileveled building of white glass and dark metal that was new to him. Inscribed large across its façade in flash-letters was THE ARCADE. Below that, in letters only a foot high, appeared—HOME OF THE BEST IN TECHNO-SEX! YOU WANT IT, WE GOT IT!

"Subtle," murmured Jake.

The bus swung into a purple-tinted parking lot next to a peach-colored restaurant and sighed gently.

"This is it, folks," announced the sombreroed robot. "We're stopping at the Hometown, USA, Café. They serve only the finest Sands BioFoods, cooked American Style. We'll be halting our tour for exactly twenty-two minutes."

As soon as the doors wooshed open, Jake was the first to disembark.

He was leaving the tour here. The Toro Plaza lay six blocks to the south and no sensible bus went anywhere near it.

The dusk was smeared with black smoke. It came swirling out of alley cookfires, went scrawling up across the fading day.

Jake had walked beyond the protection of the lights. This block was dark, most of its buildings ruined.

Propped in the doorway of a gutted apartment complex was the body of a gaunt old woman wearing the shreds of a dark overcoat. Five fat carrion crows were hopping about on her slumped corpse, pecking at her. Farther along, the body of a dead dog lay sprawled in the mouth of a sooty alley. Scrawled in glopaint on the crumbling plasbrick wall of a long defunct servo repair shop were the words BEWARE THE MAX!

Just beneath the inscription a one-legged man in a faded Mexican Army uniform sat on a crate. He glanced up at Jake with minimal interest.

Jake fished into his pocket for a coin. "What's the Max?"

The one-legged man said, "I'm not a fucking beggar, *señor.* Keep your money."

"Sorry." Jake let the coin fall back.

"The Max," said the one-legged man, "is a nickname for *Las Máquinas.*"

"And who're they?"

The one-legged man made a dry, rasping sound that might have been a laugh. "Perhaps you'll find that out tonight."

"Gives me something to look forward to." He continued on his way toward the Toro Plaza, which was still three long blocks from here.

Suddenly, overhead a white skyambulance went roaring by, belly-lights flashing red, siren hooting. In the doorway of a burned-out bodega a four-year-old boy in a ten-year-old boy's trousers stood silently bouncing a ball. His eyes didn't seem to see Jake at all.

Halfway up the next block, light showed in a few of the ground-floor windows of a ramshackle apartment house. Just before Jake reached there the door came flapping open.

A thin, dark-haired girl of no more than thirteen burst free of the building, ran down the six stone steps and into the twilit street. There was a bleeding gash across her cheek, another zigzagging along her bare shoulder. She wore a white singlet and faded blue shorts.

Stumbling, she went running across the rutted street, not noticing Jake at all.

From out of the building lunged a heavyset young man. Instead of a right hand he had a silvery knife with a ten-inch blade. "Out of the way, *cabrón,*" he said to Jake as he took off after the running girl.

She darted into a shadowy alley.

The heavyset cyborg galloped across the street, charged into the alley in her wake.

"This could be a setup," Jake reflected. "But I better make sure."

Drawing his lazgun, he headed for the alley.

Stopping at the edge of the dark alley mouth, Jake heard the sound of the girl crying out in pain and then hard metal scraping against stone.

"I won't miss again, *chiquita,*" came the voice of the cyborg. "You better just come along home with me."

"No."

The sound of running, then another cry.

Carefully Jake entered the alley. At first he saw nothing but thick darkness. Then he made out the flash of the cyborg's knifehand as it was raised high.

"Just come back, *bonita,*" he was urging. "Hey, there's only just three of us now. Rico probably isn't in the mood anymore, after the way you kicked him."

"No!"

Jake saw them now dimly. The young girl sprawled on the ground, the cyborg standing wide-legged over her. They were about fifteen feet into the alley.

Moving deeper into the darkness, Jake said, "Right about now, *amigo,* you better start moving clear of her."

The young man turned, knifehand dropping. "Didn't I tell you to keep the fuck out of this, *gringo?*"

"Just ease away from the girl." Jake had his lazgun aimed at the shadowy figure.

"You ease away, *cabrón.* This is Max business, not yours."

Halting a few feet from him, Jake ordered, "Back off. Now."

Instead the cyborg lunged at him, swinging his knifehand up.

But Jake had moved.

The blade missed, ripping only the night air.

Jake kicked out with his booted right foot, catching the knifer in the groin.

"Madre!" He started to double up.

Jake kicked again, his boot toe connecting with the cyborg's chin.

The young man jerked completely upright, as though he were trying to stretch and grow taller. His left arm slapped at his side and he produced a puzzled, whimpering noise in his throat. Then he began folding up. First at the knees, then in the middle. He hit the ground hard, flattened out, stayed there.

"Gracias," whispered the girl.

Jake dropped to one knee beside her. "Let's get you out of here. Can you walk?"

"Sí. I can—" She looked up suddenly at something above and behind Jake. *"Las Máquinas!"*

There were two more of them, climbing down the side of the building opposite. As big as the one Jake had felled, and both cyborgs, they were twenty-five feet up on a plasrod fire escape.

The nearer one had a flamegun instead of a left arm, the other a whirring saw in place of his right hand.

"You shouldn't of done that!" shouted the closer one.

Sliding an arm around the fallen girl, Jake scooped her up and started moving.

A fat line of sizzling orange flame left the cyborg's arm, cut across the alley and cooked a large black circle on the wall behind where Jake and the girl had been.

Jake fired his lazgun.

The beam sliced into the fire escape.

He fired again, slicing more of it away.

Aware of what was happening, both cyborgs tried to climb up and clear. But Jake had cut through the rickety fire escape above and below them. The center section gave way under their weight. Both came falling down.

The *Máquina* with the built-in flamegun hit first, landing with a bone-cracking thud. He kicked convulsively three times and ceased moving.

His arm jerked, spitting out a final spurt of flame. That cut across the chest of his sprawled companion and set his shirt afire.

He thrashed on the ground, screaming.

"This way quickly, *señor.*" The thin girl tugged at Jake's sleeve. "There may be more of the gang coming."

"Okay." He allowed her to lead him farther into the alley and then through a side door in one of the buildings.

"Down these steps," she said. "We can go through this cellar and get over to the next block. It's where I was trying to get to."

Nodding, Jake followed her down into the darkness.

He smelled damp earth and death.

The girl held his hand tightly, guiding him through the dark. "Sometimes people die down here. Sick people or people the cyborg gang doesn't like. That's why it stinks so."

"You live around here?"

"*Sí.*"

"Where?"

"I'm not supposed to tell—watch out, *señor.* I think I just stepped on someone."

His foot brushed against what felt like a body. "You'll have to tell me where you live. Because I'm going to see you get safely there."

"I can't go home until after ten."

"Why's that?"

She didn't answer.

He felt cool air blowing on his face.

The girl's grip on his hand tightened. "Here, up these steps."

A door creaked open and they were out on a cracked stretch of sidewalk.

"We're going to have to take care of those cuts," Jake said. "Home might be the best place to do that."

She stood close to him while she considered what he'd suggested. "My name is Strella," she said finally.

"Pleased to meet you. I'm Jake." He grinned at her. "Now, about where you live . . ."

"Well, we live at the Toro Plaza. Except that my father, who is sort of a watchman there, isn't supposed to have his family living with him. If you consider my stupid little brother and me as a family."

"And why can't you go back there yet?"

She touched, very gingerly, at the knife gash on her bare shoulder. "Once in a while my father gets involved in things that are—shady. Then he'll tell me and Janeiro, that's my stupid little brother, to go away for a while. If I hadn't been sent off tonight and then been dumb enough to wander into *Las Máquinas* territory—anyway, I'm grateful to you for coming along and helping me get away."

"What sort of shady deal is set for the Plaza tonight? Do you have any idea, Strella?"

She looked up into the night, watching a fat tourist bus go flying over. "I overheard only part of what he was saying on the phone this afternoon," she answered. "But I know it has to do with some kind of ambush. They're luring someone to the Plaza."

"And then killing him?"

Shaking her head, the girl answered, "I don't think so. My father—he's not much of a father, by the way—he said something about using a stunner and keeping the man out of sight for a few days."

"Who's going to do the job—just your father?"

"No, a son of a bitch who calls himself Sombra. He usually has two or three other assholes who work with him on his jobs."

Nodding, Jake asked her, "You can get me into the Toro Plaza without anyone noticing, can't you?"

"If I want to, *sí.*"

Jake took hold of her thin hand. "I'm pretty certain I'm the one this ambush tonight is being planned for," he told her. "I'd like, instead, to surprise Sombra."

"And my father, too," she said, laughing. "Yes, I can help you sneak in. But try not to kill my father—unless you absolutely have to."

*

The curving plasglass walls of the vast dome that sheltered the Toro Plaza had a multitude of profanity—in both Spanish and English—scrawled on them in dozens of shades of glopaint. There were all sorts of splatters and splashes as well—paint, beer, wine and blood. Up on the top of the abandoned dome pigeons and doves roosted and their droppings also decorated the walls. Hundreds of the birds were fluttering and cooing up there in the darkness now.

"We're almost to the gate we want, *señor.*" Strella was leading him along the edge of the dome, her arm linked in his.

"They're expecting me to arrive in about ten minutes."

"But they're not expecting you to turn the ambush around." The girl laughed quietly.

"Do you have any idea who Sombra is working for?"

"No, I didn't overhear anything about that." Slowing, she let go of Jake. "Here is Gate X, an old service entrance." Stopping, the girl pressed the palm of her right hand to the recog panel at the side of the wide plasglass door. "My father rigged this so it'll let me and my stupid little brother in."

Very quietly the door slid open.

Jake followed the girl into the Plaza. They were in a long, dim-lit corridor.

Strella ran silently ahead of him until she came to a black metal door marked TOROS/3. "We'll go through this storeroom," she whispered. "That'll bring us close to where Sombra ought to be waiting for you."

"Okay, fine."

She touched her hand to the black door.

After a few seconds it slid away to the right. There was a large, high room, illuminated only by a few floor-level strips of light.

Standing aside, Strella nodded at the open doorway.

Jake was one step over the threshold when the girl gave him a surprisingly powerful shove in the back.

He went staggering forward, nearly losing his balance.

He spun around just in time to see the door snap shut on him.

"Well," he observed, "this was a setup after all."

Jake noticed the bulls about ten seconds after he'd discovered that he no longer had his lazgun.

There were four of them, standing in a neat row down at the far end of the big storeroom. About three hundred feet of empty plaswood flooring separated them from Jake. Three of the robot bulls were a sleek, glistening black and the fourth was a bright scarlet.

"They're dormant, turned off," Jake said to himself after watching them for a few more seconds.

Keeping his eyes on the huge mechanical creatures anyway, he moved closer to the door. There was no way, he found, to open it from this side.

Jake next studied the walls. They were slick, made of tinted plaswood, without windows, shelves or anything to get a handhold on. The high ceiling was equally blank.

"Getting out of here's going to be tough. Especially without my gun."

Maybe he really was a little rusty after his stay up in the Freezer. He'd believed in Strella, let her convince him she was nothing more than a kid in danger. Not only had she lured him into a cage, she'd somehow managed to lift his lazgun en route.

"Could be there's a way out of here down at the other end of . . . Oops!"

The robot bulls were coming to life. The crimson one had given an angry snort, blackish smoke spewing out of his nostrils. His eyes were alive now, glowing a dazzling yellow, and with his right-front hoof he was pawing at the floor.

"Pretty obvious stuff," commented Jake, pressing back against the unopenable door. "Black smoke, flashing eyes. But I guess they figured bullfight fans'd go for that."

One of the black bulls began to move. His eyes glowed red, the smoke spewing from his nostrils was a milky white. Sparks shot up when his silvery hoof rasped at the flooring. He lowered his massive head, thick neck wrinkling, and turned to glare at Jake.

"Seems like," said Jake, "somebody wants me to learn how to be a matador."

A third robot bull was active. He began making deep roaring noises in his broad chest. Then he came toward Jake, in deliberate, mincing steps.

Jake scanned the walls again.

Not a damn thing to get a grip on, no way to climb up out of range. And nothing in the entire room to convert into a weapon.

The black bull made a nasty sound, came galloping right at Jake. His horns were made of stainless steel, the tips knife-sharp.

Waiting until the giant robot was almost on him, Jake dodged to his left.

The bull rushed by him and slammed into the wall, causing it to shudder.

"Maybe with some fancy footwork," Jake reflected, "I can avoid these guys for a while. But . . ."

The crimson bull was now trotting his way.

Apparently the fourth robot bull was defunct. At least they hadn't activated it yet. Maybe, though, they were simply saving it.

The third one was moving nearer.

Snorting out a great spume of smoke, the red bull charged Jake.

He spun suddenly, jumping back, and the bull went roaring by him with almost a foot of clearance.

Jake ran to the other side of the room. The first black bull was watching him again, about ready to make another run at him.

"Maybe I can maneuver them into crashing into each other."

He stood still, wide-legged, trying to keep track of the actions of all three of the dangerous mechanisms.

The other black one came galloping suddenly for him.

Jake sprinted over to the opposite wall.

The bull missed him.

Jake pushed off the wall before the bull could get itself turned, then he ran straight at the crimson bull.

That one lowered its head, pawed the floor and charged.

Turning, Jake started running toward the other bull.

The red bull was getting closer behind him.

Just short of the black one, Jake dived to the floor and went rolling between its legs.

He hit a wall, got to his feet.

The red bull couldn't pull up in time. It went smashing right into the black one. Its sharp metal horns stabbed into the black metal side. There came a sizzling, ratcheting sound.

Smoke came erupting out of the black bull's side, and its eyes started flashing erratically.

Easing along the wall, Jake allowed himself a nod of satisfaction. "One down," he muttered.

The two remaining bulls were both eyeing him. The surviving black one decided on another charge.

But after covering less than a third of the distance between them, it stopped dead. Its eyes clicked shut; it stood stiff and still.

The red one had also ceased to function.

A full minute passed. Then the door came whispering open.

"If you're through playing bullfighter," said Beth from the corridor, "let's go."

Jake frowned, then accepted the weapon Beth was holding out to him. It was his lazgun and he tucked it into his waistband. "How about the rest of them?" he asked her, nodding toward Strella.

The thin girl was sitting in the corridor, unconscious, slumped against the wall.

Beth held up three fingers. "There was a trio of them," she said. "I stunned two, kept the third one conscious for you to have a chat with."

Jake was looking down at Strella. "Hey, she's not breathing."

"I turned her off at their central control board—same time I shut down the bulls."

He crouched beside the frail figure. "She's an android?"

"Sure, couldn't you tell?"

"I don't have your knack." Jake straightened up.

"C'mon this way." Beth started walking along the wide corridor.

"How'd you find me?"

"If I tell you, you'll probably get angry."

"I won't, no," he promised. "But I'm curious."

Smiling as they walked along the curving corridor, she said, "When you were leaving and I hugged you—well, it wasn't just affection."

He started feeling at his back. "You planted a tracking bug on me?"

"I don't think you'll find it, Jake. It's the size of a flyspeck," Beth told him. "One I designed myself—I happened to bring a few along from the lab. It allowed me to track you, and hear everything that was going on, too. *'Gracias,* dear *señor.* Oh, you have saved me from a fate worse than death.' Boy, Jake, how could you fall for such—"

"You had to have been there. She was very convincing."

Beth glanced at him. "Maybe I shouldn't have planted that thing on you, but I just didn't like the sound of this meeting setup. Soon as you left, I took off in our skycar."

Jake was silent for a few seconds. "No, that was a good idea," he said eventually. "We're partners, after all. I've got to keep that in mind from now on."

Beth laughed. "You're mellowing."

"A brisk workout with a few bulls tends to do that to me."

"I'm sorry I couldn't get them deactivated sooner."

"Listen, I think I was winning when you got here," he said. "Another few minutes and—"

"You wouldn't have beaten the fourth one. He's rigged to breathe out flame." Beth stopped at an open doorway. "In here."

On the slick white floor at the far side of the room lay two men, both unconscious. One on his back, one on his stomach. Monitor screens ringed the walls, and at the room's center was a complex control board. In front of it, tied in a plaschair, was Jake's contact here in Cuidado.

"I guess," said the fat Globo, "you'd like an explanation, huh, Jake?"

"That'd be nice." Jake's grin was not a warm one.

The fat man wiped at his perspiring forehead. "This was strictly a monetary thing, you understand," he was explaining.

Jake was straddling a chair five feet from him. "Selling somebody out usually involves money. Go on."

"Keep in mind that you and I were never close friends. So it isn't as though I'm a Judas or—"

"What were you supposed to do?"

Globo gave his forehead another nervous swipe. "This is going to sound pretty awful to you."

"Tell me anyway."

The fat man mumbled something inaudible.

Beth was leaning against the wall, hands in the hip pockets of her trousers. "We didn't catch that. *Otra vez, por favor.*"

Looking up at her, Globo answered, "I was hired to kill him."

"By whom?" she asked.

Starting to wad up his handkerchief, he said, "Keep in mind that I was paid a considerable sum."

"Who?" asked Jake.

"Vargas."

"Rafe Vargas."

"That one, *sí.*"

Jake studied him for a few silent seconds. "Vargas is Warbride's lover and second in command. Why's he want me dead?"

"It's not a military thing at all, Jake." He wadded the handkerchief up even tighter. "Vargas is aware that you and Warbride were once . . . good friends."

"Not exactly that."

Globo concentrated on his fat fingers as they poked and pressed at the damp handkerchief. "The man is very jealous. He doesn't want you getting near the lady again," he said. "Once he learned I was seeking to arrange a meeting between you and Warbride, he had me contacted."

"Who did that?"

"A nobody, a go-between. His name I don't even know."

Jake rubbed at his chin. "You're telling me that Warbride herself doesn't even know anything about this?"

"Sí, nada."

Jake glanced over at Beth. "What do you think?"

"He's too scared to be lying."

"Exactly, *señorita,* obviously." He used the handkerchief again on his sweating forehead. "The truth is what I'm telling you."

Standing, slowly, Jake crossed over to Beth. "Now we have to find another way to arrange a meeting with Warbride."

"I can still help you with that," offered Globo. "It would be an honor to—"

"Nope. I'll make other arrangements." Jake borrowed Beth's stungun from her, turned and used it on the fat man.

The robot madam greeted Jake warmly. She was tall and wide with an ample chrome-plated bosom showing beneath her shimmering glogold dress. "Been one hell of a long time, Jake honey," she boomed as she gave him another enthusiastic hug. Her plump chrome cheeks were decorated with glimmering gems, her crinkly blonde hair was made of spun gold, and she smelled strongly of a dozen different flowers. "I heard you were out of the snoozer, but I didn't think I'd see you down here at the Arcade."

Extricating himself, politely, from her exuberant embrace, Jake took two backward steps across the ivory-colored parlor rug. "You seem to be thriving down here, Mama Reina."

Chuckling, she returned to her huge lucite rocking chair. "We got the most successful high-tech whorehouse this side of the border," she told him as she resumed rocking. "But since when did you go in for andyhookers?"

"I don't," he replied. "I'm looking for a friend of mine who's supposed to be here."

"Aw now, honey, I hate to interrupt a customer."

"He's not a customer. This guy's a reporter with *GLA Week*—Ogden Swires."

"Him, yeah. He's doing a story on the Arcade." She chuckled, slapping at one chrome knee. "That faxzine is supposed to have a readership of around four million, so an article there'll be great publicity. You just came down from GLA, didn't you? How many of those four million you figure are frustrated and horny?"

"Most all of them."

"Exactly, so a story in that rag of Swires' will boost business. Local color and nookie's a great combination." She ceased rocking, pushed down on the arms of her chair and shoved to a standing position. "I've put on a lot of weight since I knew you in GLA, honey."

"How's that?"

"Hell, I had to have lots of extra security gadgets built in," explained Mama Reina. "Tourists get a lot goofier than locals. But now I'm equipped to stun them, tranquilize them and even perform a little minor surgery if need be. I can also clear a Banx card in less than thirty seconds."

"Notice you've added some new rubies, too."

Smiling, the robot madam tapped her cheek. "Yeah, the gift of an admirer. I got some swell new diamonds, too, but they don't show when I'm wearing this dress," she said, waddling toward the door. "Your newshound buddy's in the Voyeur Lounge. I'll personally escort you there, lover."

There were one hundred and twenty large vidmonitor screens built into the milky plasglass walls of the large, oval Voyeur Lounge. Four tiers of three-foot-square screens, each with a wide, gilded catwalk for guests who wanted to stroll. At various spots along each catwalk comfortable airchairs were placed for those who wanted to enjoy an extended view of the activity on any particular screen.

The black *GLA* reporter was up on the second level, walking slowly along and muttering into the recorder-mike in his hand. Something like thirty customers were enjoying the screens on the four tiers.

"Hey, Chop Suey," shouted Mama Reina at a Chinese tourist

who was aiming his camera at a row of viewscreens. "You were supposed to check your goddamn camera. No pictures allowed in here—so hand it over pronto."

"I wasn't informed of this," he replied, leaning out over the golden railing on the third level. "Being an accredited sociologist and not some perverse thrill-seeker, I intend to employ my camera until—"

"Nuts." The big robot swung up her right arm and aimed a chrome forefinger at his chest.

A thin, crackling beam of greenish light shot out of the tip of the metal finger, hitting the Chinese square in the forehead. He gasped, teetered for about nine seconds and then came falling down toward the floor.

Mama Reina scooted swiftly over, caught the unconscious customer before he smacked the silvery carpeting, dumped him on the nearest sofa. Smiling at Jake, she tromped on the fallen camera with her spiked heel. "No pictures, you dinks," she announced to the rest of the voyeurs.

They returned to their viewing.

Giving the robot madam a nod of thanks, Jake climbed up to the second tier.

"On Screen 42 there's an overweight, pudgy man of nearly fifty enjoying freefall sex with two silver-plated nymphet androids," Swires was dictating into his recorder. "Screen 43 shows us a fat, middle-aged lady being tied to a painbed by a naked male android wearing a sombrero." He glanced over at the approaching Jake. "About breakfast."

"It's okay, you were tired." Jake grinned. "No need to apologize, Og, for falling asleep in the middle of the meal."

"I wasn't tired." He clicked off the recorder, let his hand swing down to his side. "I make it a point to get sufficient sleep, even when I'm covering a war."

"Whatever your reasons for passing out, Miss Kittridge wasn't offended. So let's simply forget it."

Swires eyed him. "I've done some checking since you ditched me, Jake." He slumped into one of the white airchairs. "You're working for Bascom's Cosmos outfit these days. You're supposed to be finding the missing Professor Kittridge and his daughter. Seems you've already located Beth Kittridge, so why the hell are you hanging around Cuidado?"

"There's still her dad to locate."

"Did she hypnotize me?"

"Nope, and she didn't drug you either. Neither did I. You really, simply—dozed off."

"There's something odd going on. I can sense it."

"I hear you've been cleared to cross over into Chihuahua to interview Warbride."

"How'd you find that out? I only just—"

"I want to see her, too. But my initial contact fell through."

Swires was distracted by one of the voyeur screens. "Romancing somebody in a vat full of mud doesn't appeal to me. But then neither does the idea of watching somebody romancing somebody in a vat of mud. For that matter, I don't see the fun in romancing somebody in a vat full of mud and knowing that somebody's watching me over a video monitor. I tell you, Jake, if I didn't need this story, I'd pack my gear and go back to my hotel to wash my—"

"You're due to take off in the morning for the Warbride interview. I'd like to come along."

The reporter frowned at him. "How come, Jake? You're supposed to be a former gentleman friend of the lady's. You ought to be able to drop in on her anytime you want."

"I have to see her right now. There isn't time to wait for a message to get to Warbride and back."

"What about the Kittridge girl?" Swires narrowed one eye. "Is she coming along, too?"

"She is, yeah, if that's okay with you."

"And I can interview her?"

"Sure," promised Jake, "but not until after we find her father."

"Maybe you'll ditch me again and I won't get a damn thing."

"You'll get a story, Og. But not yet."

Swires watched another of the screens for a few seconds. "I never found fat women that attractive. And two fat naked andies don't do anything for me."

"If things turn out as I expect," said Jake, "you're going to get a damn good story out of this."

"When I knew you up in GLA a few years ago, you were pretty honest," said Swires. "I could trust you."

"You still can."

"Okay, be at my hotel in the morning at seven sharp, you and the young lady," he said, rising. "But, Jake, if at any point along the way I find myself dozing off unexpectedly for even a minute, the deal's off."

Beth wasn't in her room when Jake returned to the inn.

Standing in the open doorway between their rooms, he called her name.

After a moment the sliding door in his room opened.

He spun, reaching for the lazgun at his waist.

"Only me," said the dark-haired young woman as she stepped in out of the early morning.

Jake relaxed, letting go of the gun butt. "I was concerned about you."

Smiling, she sat on the edge of his bed. "I was only outside," she said. "I like to do that when I'm by myself. Sit out in the open and just think about things. I've done that ever since I was a kid. When we used to visit my uncle's chateau on the moon, I'd—"

"Be better if you kept out of sight when I'm not around."

"Yes, sir."

"Okay, I'm not trying to sound like your official guardian." He sat in the vinyl armchair. "But we do seem to have several different groups who'd like to do one or both of us in."

"Do you think Rafe Vargas is really jealous of you?"

"Meaning he might have a less romantic reason for trying to get me killed?"

Beth nodded. "Not that you aren't a formidable rival, Jake. But, yes," she said. "It might be that Vargas, despite his closeness to your old friend Warbride, is linked up with someone else."

"Such as Sonny Hokori or one of the other Tek kingpins."

"Yes, or possibly even Bennett Sands," she said. "I have a vague impression that I heard him discuss Vargas with my father once."

Linking his fingers, Jake rested his chin on them. "Let's keep that in mind when we meet Vargas."

"You've arranged a way to get us across to Warbride?"

"Yeah, but I had to promise Ogden Swires an exclusive interview with you."

Her eyes widened. "We're going with him?"

"He got his okay to cross into Chihuahua. Seems to me it's a fairly safe way of getting to Warbride. I don't trust any of my contacts hereabouts."

"But you trust Swires?"

"A lot more than I trust people like Globo."

"I'll be evasive as possible," she said. "Does he know I put him to sleep?"

"He suspects, but I tried to divert him from that notion."

"Where'd you find him?"

Jake stood, stretching. "Around town."

"Where specifically?"

He turned to look out into the three A.M. darkness. "The Arcade, doing a story."

After a few seconds she asked, "When's the last time you were in Cuidado?"

"Something like seven years ago."

"Did you ever travel here with your father?"

"I never traveled anywhere with my father."

"I thought you lived with him in Mexico."

"When he was stationed in Mexico City, back when I was in my late teens, we shared a house," Jake said, still not looking at her. "We didn't socialize much."

"How old were you when your mother died?"

"I forget," he said. "Around sixteen or seventeen."

"Were you all living together then?"

"Nope, she was in GLA—he was stationed in Central America someplace—I was going to school up at a place called the Sky Academy."

"That's supposed to be a very good school."

"Very good for troublesome boys."

"Were you?"

"He thought so."

"And your mother?"

"She was sick by that time and didn't get to vote."

"Still, going to school in an orbiting colony like the Sky Academy must've been fun."

"Almost as much fun as the Freezer." He turned and faced her. "We have to meet Swires at seven in the morning. You don't need sleep, but I do."

She left the bed, standing straight. "Yes, I keep forgetting. Sorry. Shall I wake you around six?"

"No need, thanks. Good night."

Passing him on the way to her doorway, she paused and kissed him on the cheek. "Good night."

The landvan drove itself. A small black guidebox had been attached to the dash control-panel, and that took care of driving the battered vehicle through the hot, dry countryside.

The aircirc system functioned only intermittently, and the plasglass windows refused to open. By midday the interior of the van was too warm and the scents of the previous cargoes and passengers had grown thicker.

"All around us stretch sad scenes of devastation . . ." Swires, seated in the driveseat, was dictating into his recorder-mike. "This village we're passing through now, wherein some of the fiercest fighting in all of the Chihuahua rebellion took place but scant weeks ago, is like the gutted skeleton of lost hopes. Many of its humble cottages and shops are blackened, fallen-down ruins. Its hollow-eyed denizens wander like forlorn sleepwalkers, and circling in the glaring sky like lost punctuation marks are the ebony scavenger birds who await a chance to descend and—"

"You used that phrase before," mentioned Jake, who was slouched in the passenger seat closest to the right side-window.

"Twice, in fact," added Beth, who sat beside him with her long legs tucked under her.

"Have I?" The *GLA Week* reporter clicked off his recorder-mike. "That happens to me sometimes when I get too emotionally involved with my subject."

"How did you get involved?" asked Jake. "We've been rolling through Chihuahua locked up tight inside this van. Haven't stopped, haven't talked to anybody."

"I'm a sensitive observer. When I see what the civil war has done to this area, it touches me. I don't have to get out and roll around in the muck."

The van swerved to avoid a dead horse in the wide, dusty roadway that cut through the center of the town. Then, rattling and chuffing, it turned onto a side road.

Beth asked, "What time did you say we're supposed to reach our first rendezvous spot?"

"The fellow who delivered this robot van to me told me that'd be around one P.M.," Swires told her.

"Then we ought to be just about there."

Jake said, "We look to be heading for the back country."

There were no more houses now, only dry yellow fields on each side of the narrow, twisting road. Scattered across a burned-out stretch of land were the remains of three big gray combat robots. Arms, legs, torsos, heads, blackened and twisted.

The van slowed, swung sharply to the left and hopped off the road. It went bumping over a ditch and into a flat, yellow field. The engine turned itself off and, after producing a few final pings, the vehicle grew silent.

"Apparently," said Beth, stretching her legs out in front of her, "we've arrived."

The air a hundred feet directly in front of them started to shimmer. Slowly, with occasional jerks, a building began to take shape. It was a large, sprawling hacienda with seemingly thick adobe walls and slanting red tile roofs. Lush shrubbery sprouted up in front of the hologram house, and a wide red brick path appeared, leading to its polished oaken door.

"Impressive," observed Swires.

"So's this," said Jake, nodding to his right.

Five dark men in tan uniforms that were trimmed with scarlet were standing close to Jake's side of the halted landvan. Four of them held lazrifles pointed at the passengers.

"Less flippancy in your answers, if you don't mind." The captain took one precise step forward and slapped Beth hard across the face.

"Damn you." Jake started to lunge at him.

"It's okay, Jake." She caught his arm, holding him back. "Easy now."

He subsided, but the deepened lines remained across his forehead.

The man who'd hit Beth was small and thin, about fifty. His left eye was circled with scar tissue and frozen in a perpetual wink. He'd introduced himself as Captain Aguilar. "Let me explain what's going on," he told them. "We have good reason to believe that an attempt is going to be made on our leader's life. These would-be assassins of Warbride are supposedly going to be posing as foreign journalists."

"I'm certainly not an assassin," insisted Swires. "You've checked every damn item in my ID packet. Hey, you even confirmed my ret patterns with that unsanitary retina-scanner your sergeant lugs around in his knapsack."

"Quite possibly you are who you claim to be, Señor Swires," acknowledged the captain. "This outspoken young woman, however, has absolutely no identification at all."

"I was involved in a crash," she said. "Everything was lost."

"You claim to be Beth Kittridge?"

"I am Beth Kittridge."

The captain shook his head. "That seems to me very unlikely."

Jake asked him, "Why—do you have some reason for believing otherwise?"

"And you, Señor Cardigan, are a convicted criminal who purports to be an employee of a North American detective agency which itself has a highly unsavory reputation." He shook his head even more vigorously. "You also have a most unfortunate attitude."

Swires gave an exasperated groan. "*Oigame, por favor*—my interview with Warbride was set up by your own publicity rep," he informed the small captain. "I sat around on my toke in Cuidado for days waiting for all the damn rigamarole to get itself—"

"You're in a war zone here," reminded Aguilar. "What some effete public relations person may have promised you back in the safety of—"

"What's the hacienda for?" Jake pointed at it with a thumb.

Captain Aguilar said, "Señor Cardigan—if indeed that is who you really are—*por favor,* don't interrupt me again."

Jake was looking him up and down. "I think I used to know you, Aguilar," he said thoughtfully. "Sure . . . you used to be a pimp for rebuilt andy hookers up in Tijuana back about—"

"That will be enough—*basta!*" The captain raised his hand to strike Jake, then decided against it. "You'll all remain here, under guard, until certain officials in Warbride's provisional government arrive to take over your questioning. The hacienda, *señor,* is for that purpose."

"When will they get here?" asked Swires.

"Quién sabe?" Shrugging, Captain Aguilar walked away. The four others stayed where they were, ringing them, with lazrifles in hand.

Beth leaned close to Jake. "Was he really a pimp?"

"Yep, he was. As I recollect—and this was quite a time ago—I arrested him at least twice."

"That sure isn't," complained Swires, "going to help our case."

The gleaming black landcar came driving into the field late in the afternoon. Its windows were blank and there was not a single speck of dust on its entire bright surface.

Captain Aguilar and the four other soldiers snapped to attention.

Jake was squatting near the believable projection of a brick pathway. Beth was sitting, legs crossed, right on the path itself, and spoiling a portion of the illusion. Swires was spread out on the ground and resting on one arm, his back to the flowering shrubs that bordered the front of the hacienda.

Rising to his feet, Jake watched the long dark car roll to a stop some thirty feet away.

Aguilar moved toward the rear of the vehicle. He clicked his heels and bowed as a blind door hissed slowly open. "General Ribera, sir, welcome." Bowing once more, he then stepped back to salute again.

A tall, slender man in a cream-colored suit emerged from the car.

"These three are the suspected assassins," explained the captain, gesturing at them.

Ribera was staring right at Jake. He started laughing. "What the hell are you up to now, Jake?"

"Eddie . . . How long have you been a general?"

Swires popped upright. "Things are looking up," he remarked.

The general and Jake were in what appeared to be a large, wood-paneled living room. Ribera was perched on an upturned plascrate. Jake was pacing.

"Quit wandering around, Jake. You kick up dust and shatter the illusion."

"You set up one of these hologram haciendas wherever you go?"

"No, but Aguilar likes to. I find it best to humor him in small things."

Halting, Jake asked, "When did you quit being a lawyer up in the Borderland?"

"Nearly five years ago," answered his friend. "Then—it happened while you were away—I decided to join with Warbride. You haven't kept up with the political situation here in the country, but things have been growing much worse. President Romero is a charming lady—though nowhere near as tough or practical as Warbride—but she's allowed those around her to step up the oppression and . . . Ah, but there's no need for an oration. Tell me what brings you here?"

"I came to see Warbride."

"To rekindle your former—"

"Jesus, Eddie, just about everybody in Mexico seems to think that she and I had one of the great romances of the century." Jake spread his hands wide. "But it wasn't that at all. I have to see her now because of a case I'm working on."

"Police business?"

Grinning, Jake replied, "I'm out of the Freezer, but not off the shitlist. No, I'm a private operative now—working for the Cosmos Detective Agency in GLA."

Ribera said, "Not a bad outfit. Bascom isn't exactly honest, but he's not a rascal like some of his competitors. What does our mutual friend have to do with the case?"

"Cosmos was hired to locate Professor Kittridge and his daughter."

Slowly General Ribera stood. "That's who the young woman outside is—I thought I recognized her," he said. "Doesn't she know where her father is?"

"Nope. Do you?"

Ribera turned half away from him, watching Jake through narrowed eyes. "What is it—you suspect Warbride is involved in the professor's disappearance?"

"There was apparently a crash and it took place in the *Selva Grande,* which she now controls." Jake started to pace again and yellow dust swirled up through the floorboards. "And among the several attempts to knock me off that have occurred since I crossed the border—at least one was arranged by people close to her."

Ribera held up his right hand, palm toward Jake. "No, that isn't true. There's been no order to harm you or anyone around you."

"Does Vargas need her okay to try something like that?"

"Ah—Vargas . . ."

"I'm pretty certain he gave orders to have me killed, Eddie."

"My relationship with Warbride is not without problems," admitted the general. "One of them is Rafe Vargas. She and I don't agree as to his worth or his loyalty."

"So he could be behind the attempt?"

"Most certainly, *sí.*"

Jake stopped close to his friend. "You have no idea what happened to Professor Kittridge?"

"None whatsoever, no." He put a hand on Jake's shoulder. "But I'll arrange for you to get safely to Warbride's camp."

Jake said, "*Bueno.*"

At dusk they reached the Great Forest. The huge trees rose up hundreds of feet and stretched away ahead of them like endless rows of giant pillars. Darkness was slowly starting to fill in the spaces between the trees, and their high, distant branches seemed to be fading.

General Ribera, who was driving the black landcar, stopped at the edge of the wide roadway that went cutting through the *Selva Grande.* "Yet another checkpoint," he remarked.

Three uniformed men, each armed with a lazrifle, had been leaning against the trunk of a single immense tree. They snapped to attention and one of them came trotting over to the halted car.

"*Buenas noches,* General," the soldier said after looking in at the open window.

"We're heading for the central encampment, Corporal," Ribera informed him.

"You can pass on, General Ribera." Stepping back, the man saluted.

"That's Carlos Troxa, isn't it?" Jake inquired as the window hissed shut and the landcar began moving again. He was sitting in the passenger seat next to his friend.

"The corporal's name is Troxa, I believe, yes. Why?"

"I remember him from the Borderland—used to be a pickpocket. Not a major one."

Ribera smiled. "A cause can reform a man, Jake."

"Maybe. Sometimes."

"You're even more cynical than you used to be."

"I probably am, yes."

From the backseat Ogden Swires said, "Tyranny has an uplifting and ennobling effect. It turns thieves and ne'er-do-wells into patriots in the service of a worthy cause."

"Beg pardon?" said Ribera.

"He's only dictating something for his story," explained Beth, who was sharing the backseat with the reporter.

Swires asked, "When am I going to be allowed to take some pictures, General?"

"When we reach the base."

"But I'd really like to get some shots of this forest. The trees are really quite—"

"That isn't possible, *señor.* We don't want any specific details of the route to the camp appearing."

"I can be very discreet in snapping the—"

"It's not permitted."

Sighing, Swires returned to talking quietly into his recorder-mike.

Jake asked, "What exactly have you heard about Professor Kittridge's crash, Eddie?"

"Nothing beyond the fact that a crash apparently occurred."

They were surrounded now by the giant trees, and the day was moving rapidly toward night.

Jake said, "But their skycruiser came down fairly near here."

"Supposedly, yes."

"Supposedly? Do you have doubts?"

"I mean only that I was away at the time, Jake. Therefore I possess nothing but hearsay information." Ribera glanced briefly back at Beth. "Surely the *señorita* can provide you with all the details, since she was with her father."

"Actually I wasn't," she said.

"I heard that—"

"She wasn't," Jake interrupted. "Is there anything else you can add?"

Shaking his head, Ribera said, "No, nothing . . . *nada.*"

"You know Bennett Sands."

"Of course. Though I'm not overly fond of him," the general admitted. "I must mention, however, that he's been most helpful to us."

"How so?"

"He's given Warbride considerable financial aid."

"To make certain," Beth said, resting her hand on the headrest of Jake's seat, "that his own holdings hereabouts don't get damaged or nationalized."

The general said, "That may well be his motive."

"Then Warbride might," said Jake, "do Sands a favor."

"She might. What sort do you have in mind, Jake?"

"Don't know. Something to do with Kittridge, probably."

Ribera nodded. "*Sí,* that's possible."

"But she wouldn't necessarily confide in you if she had?"

Ribera laughed. "You know her," he said. "Warbride is not the confiding type—not with her lovers and not with her generals."

The noise came rolling through the night forest, hundreds of voices shouting and one amplified voice booming out above them. There was a glare, too, starting to show up ahead.

Landcars were parked at the side of the wide woodland road, landvans as well, and even some jetcycles.

Pulling off the road, Ribera said, "I'd forgotten about this. We'll stop here and go the rest of the way on foot."

"What's going on?" asked Jake.

"A sort of rally." The general got out of the car. "Warbride's addressing her followers—and the event's being vidtaped."

"Propaganda, huh?" Jake joined him at the side of the road.

"Copies of the vidtape will be circulated."

Swires asked, "Can I use my camera now?"

Smiling faintly, Ribera replied, "No one will object, *señor.*"

Beth took Jake's arm. "Vargas is likely to be here, isn't he?" she asked quietly.

"I sure hope so."

She tightened her grip on his arm. "I don't think this is the ideal location for confronting him."

The shouting from up ahead grew louder, and then there was a sudden and abrupt silence.

Five seconds passed.

The amplified voice of a woman came echoing through the great trees. "Who am I?"

"Warbride," answered the as-yet-unseen crowd.

"I cannot hear you."

"*Warbride!*"

"Once again, please. I still can't quite hear you."

"WARBRIDE!"

"I have been called Warbride since I was seventeen. Since my brother and father vanished. Since they were made to disappear because they believed in freedom—not just freedom for themselves, but for all of Mexico. They vanished because they opposed the ruthless tyrant who then ruled our country . . ."

With Ribera in the lead, they made their way toward the rally. There were more cars now, more landvans, more jetcycles, all crowded at the sides of the roadway. The bright white light coming from up ahead made the parked vehicles gleam and glow.

". . . and that man, that despot, was not as bad as the whore who occupies our capital now. I have been called Warbride since the day I was raped by federal soldiers. Raped by five men who served a tyrant. I have been Warbride since that day. Since that dark day when I swore that I would marry not a lover, not a good man who wanted me—I would be married to *war!* And I shall remain the bride of war and revolution until my country—until *our* country—is free. Tell me my name."

"Warbride!"

"*Warbride!*"

"WARBRIDE!"

Gigantic trees had been cut down, at least two dozen of them to make a large clearing. There appeared to be well over a thousand people, men and women, in uniform and out, seated on the bare ground and all staring at a wide, raised, wooden platform. On each side of the platform stood a huge vidscreen, each one twenty-five feet high and twenty-five feet wide. A dark-haired woman, wearing tan trousers, highly polished black boots and a blood-red sleeveless tunic, stood alone on the stage. On both screens there showed an enormous image of her. She wore her hair cut short, and there were traces of weariness and strain showing in her tanned face. She was a pretty woman, with an intensity in her dark eyes. She raised her right hand and her arm flashed and glittered in the spotlights aimed at her. It was chrome-plated metal to just below the elbow.

Beth leaned closer to Jake and whispered, "She looks a lot older than I expected."

"Careful where you step," Ribera cautioned as he led them up to the bright-lit clearing.

"Holograms," realized Jake, scanning the rear rows of the audience.

"It helps make for a more convincing propaganda vidfilm," the general said. "We actually have only about four hundred in attendance, but a thousand looks better and—ah, *señor,* I'd prefer if you didn't photograph this particular aspect of our rally."

Swires, crouching slightly, was about to use his small pixcam. "These projected people'll come out looking nearly real in my—"

"Even so."

Reluctantly, the reporter lowered his camera. "I'm going to have to sacrifice my reputation for bringing my readers nothing but the truth," he complained.

Ribera said, "We can sit back here, Jake, until Warbride's finished speaking. Then I'll take you to her." He squatted on the ground, just behind a very believable row of holograms.

Jake sat, beckoning Beth down next to him. "Warbride's a good five years younger than I am," he told her.

"That doesn't exactly make her a teenager." She settled cross-legged beside him. "You've held up a lot better."

"Been getting a lot of rest lately."

Up on the platform Warbride was saying, "We must be loyal not just to the flag and the other beloved symbols of our country, we must be loyal to the *idea* of Mexico. And that idea cannot be the idea of one person, nor of a dictator or of that bitch who calls herself president. Mexico must be the idea of all of us. Mexico is what you think and feel and what you want for yourselves and for your children. Mexico is all of us—all of the fifteen hundred loyal warriors, men and women, who've journeyed here tonight, and all of you who will hear my words and see my image."

She raised her metal arm again, and for several seconds a gigantic image of it flashed on both the great screens.

"There is no room among us for anyone who is not loyal," she continued. "Our cause is too important for that. Anyone who is disloyal to me—and, therefore, to you and to Mexico—must die."

"Damn," said Ribera. "She promised me there'd be no more of these."

"A public execution?" asked Jake.

"Yes—and that makes us no better than President Romero."

Someone was being led out onto the stage now. His pale blue suit was tattered, splashed with blood. His face was bruised and cut.

But Jake recognized him. "That's Globo." He got to his feet.

"Jake, stay here," urged Beth, reaching up and grabbing his sleeve.

"Globo, poor bastard, was disloyal to me if anybody," he said. "He's being killed now to keep him quiet."

"But you can't go—"

"Sure I can." Shaking free of her grasp, Jake started walking through the crowd toward the platform.

The crowd became aware that Jake was striding toward the platform. They grew silent for a moment, then began murmuring.

One of the small botcameras that was hovering over the clearing came gliding down to get a look at him.

The murmuring of the several hundred real soldiers grew louder. But since they were uncertain as to whether or not Jake was part of the show, no one made a move to stop him.

When he was still about a hundred feet from the bright-lit platform, Warbride came to its edge and, shielding her eyes with her flesh hand, stared out at him.

It took her another ten seconds to realize who he was. Then she smiled in recognition and the smile was flashed large on the screens. "Jake, *cariño,*" she said, laughing. "It's been a very long time."

"It has," he agreed, stopping a few feet short of the platform and looking up at her.

She pointed skyward with her metal thumb. "You were away—and frankly I didn't expect you'd be out this soon. Nor, *mi alma,* that you'd show up here."

"I've been trying to see you," he said to her. "But apparently that news hasn't gotten to you."

"No, no one told me that—"

"We have business to attend to," cut in a harsh, grating voice from Jake's right.

From behind one of the huge picture screens stepped a tall, wide-shouldered man. He wore a tight-fitting uniform, and spread across his broad chest were dozens of medals and ribbons. He was about forty and a little more than half of his face was handsome. The rest of it had been replaced by silvery metal. His left hand was metal, too, of the same gleaming silver.

"General Vargas!" cried someone in the crowd.

Others shouted the name. "Vargas!"

Turning, Jake said, "I've been wanting to run into you, Vargas."

"And I've been most anxious to encounter you, Señor Cardigan." Stopping a few feet short of Jake, Vargas gave him a slight, stiff bow. "First, though, I must take care of this traitor."

"Kill the traitor!" shouted a good portion of the crowd.

On the platform, held by two soldiers, the sweating fat man was watching Jake and the general.

"The thing is," said Jake, "I don't think Globo's been disloyal to Warbride's cause. He set me up, sure, but that should've earned him a—"

"It's extremely dangerous," warned Vargas, "to intercede in an official execution, *señor.*" From his silver-trimmed leather holster he drew a long-barreled lazgun. "If you will step aside now, I—"

"Jake, why are you so interested in this traitor?" Warbride had detached her mikes, was sitting on the edge of the platform and gazing down at the two men.

"Have you questioned Globo?"

"Of course not—I don't participate in that sort of thing anymore."

"Be interesting if you did, since I think Vargas doesn't want Globo to talk about what he's been up to lately."

"I don't understand, *cariño.*"

"Don't you really know that Vargas hired Globo to have me killed?"

She frowned at the general. *"Es verdad?"*

"Obviously not." Vargas raised the gun to take aim at Globo.

Jake moved then.

He sprinted forward, across the gap between himself and the cyborg. His right hand chopped at the gun in the metal fingers. He knocked it free of Vargas' grasp.

"Another traitor!" Several soldiers in the front row started to rise up.

"Back!" ordered Warbride, standing.

Vargas swung at Jake with his metal hand.

He hit Jake just below the breastbone, causing him to gasp and go staggering back.

Vargas followed him, striking him against the side of the head.

The harsh light of the clearing seemed to flare suddenly brighter.

Jake fell to one knee.

Vargas stood over him, raising his metal fist to strike him again.

But Jake made a lunge, butting the cyborg in the midsection.

Vargas coughed out air. He stumbled back, lost his balance, fell to his side in the dirt.

Jake charged, threw himself on the fallen man and started jabbing him in the ribs.

"Stop!" ordered Warbride from the platform.

Both men ignored her, rolling over as they struggled.

Jake caught a glimpse of Warbride's metal arm pointing down at them. Then a thin, glittering line of green light jumped from her forefinger.

It cut through the night and hit Vargas in the face. The silver side of it made a sizzling sound and his whole body jerked. His metal fingers came clawing up to scratch at his face. Then he jerked once more and was still.

Jake pushed himself up off the ground, started to turn toward the platform.

The beam hit him in the chest.

He felt as though he were being lifted clear off the ground. The most important thing in the world was to get one more breath of air. But he could no longer breathe; he was frozen and couldn't move. All the light went away.

*

He heard the wind. It was blowing harsh and hard outside wherever he was.

Jake slowly awakened. He was flat on his back on a wide, carved-wood bed, and his skeleton inside him felt as though it had been taken apart and then reassembled not quite correctly.

Pushing backward with both elbows, he managed to get himself into a sitting position atop the antique bed.

The night wind rattled the high, wide, plasglass windows that circled the dim-lit room. All that showed outside were the clear dark sky, stars and a pale half-moon.

He grimaced, shook his head, carefully, from side to side. He still enjoyed awakening, even though right now he had to undergo the discomforting aftereffects of having been knocked out with a stunbeam.

"Got one built into that arm of hers," he said as he attempted to slide clear of the bed and stand up. "Very convenient for her."

Stepping onto the thickly carpeted floor caused, for some reason, all his teeth to ache for a while. There were also assorted twinges making themselves known in his elbows and knees and along his ribs.

Doing it very gradually, Jake walked over to one of the windows. That produced a whole new set of aches and pains.

He was in a tower, very high up. The treetops of the *Selva Grande* showed about fifty feet below. They were swaying in the strong wind.

"This must be," Jake decided, "one of the ranger stations. Taken over and redecorated by Warbride."

Small plasglass panels had been set in the pale pink walls here and there around the room, and they glowed with a faint rose-colored light. The carpeting was pale pink and so was the only door.

Inhaling deeply, Jake started for the door.

It slid silently open before he was closer than ten feet to it.

Framed in the brighter, harsher light of the corridor was Warbride. Hands on hips, she stood smiling at him. She was dressed as she had been at the rally.

"I'm truly sorry, *caro,* that I had to incapacitate you for—" She glanced at the tiny watch built into her chrome arm. "For nearly four hours. But I wanted to cool you off—you and Rafe both."

"You succeeded, Elana."

Her smile broadened and she crossed the threshold. She walked up to him, put her arms around him and kissed him full on the mouth. "You remember my name," she said finally.

Easing back from her, he said, "Would you prefer I shouted 'Warbride' a few times?"

Crossing to the bed, she sat on its edge. "The rally was—a political necessity, Jake."

"I especially liked the story about how you got your nickname."

Laughing, Warbride said, "My speechwriter came up with that six months ago—and it really seems to have quite an effect on audiences. He used to be a professor of literature at Mexico University, before that whore, President Romero, put his name on a death list. Originally I was saying I was raped by three soldiers. I decided five sounds better."

Jake watched her. "It was also interesting to find out how your brother Jorge disappeared. I'd always thought he went into hiding to avoid being nabbed for dealing Tek."

She shrugged one shoulder, brushed at her short-cropped hair with her silvery metal fingers. "We changed poor Jorge's bio for propaganda reasons," she said. "A martyr is better than a fugitive from the law."

"I think you can help me, Elana."

"Ah, then you didn't come here to rekindle—"

"Whatever we had once, Elana, is long gone."

"*Muy triste,*" she said with a sigh. "But also true, alas. What is it you need, Jake?"

"I'm working for the Cosmos Detective Agency, and they—"

"No longer a policeman," she said, shaking her head. "I always thought that was a lifetime calling for you, Juanito."

"So did I—once." He went over to sit beside her. "Cosmos wants to find Professor Leon Kittridge and his daughter. Their skycruiser is supposed to have crashed near here a couple of—"

"You're traveling with the Kittridge girl, which strikes me as very strange. Yet you say that you are searching for her and—"

"She's not Beth Kittridge."

"Isn't she? From pictures I've—"

"Where is she now, by the way?"

Smiling, Warbride pointed at the floor with her metal forefinger. "Perfectly safe, Jake," she assured him, "in a guest room two levels down. That *niña* is very fond of you—and she was very unhappy with me for stunning you."

"What about the Kittridge skycruiser?"

"I was told that it did crash here in the *Selva Grande.*"

"You didn't see the wreckage?"

"No, but Rafe Vargas did."

"What happened to Kittridge and his daughter?"

"Both dead," said Warbride.

Jake went over to stare out into the clear black night. The wind was blowing harder. "I don't think they're dead," he said, "because too many people are still trying to keep me from finding them."

"Maybe it's only that you don't want to believe the truth."

"The truth, Elana, isn't something I expect to get from Vargas."

"Just because I used the stunbeam on him tonight, *caro,* doesn't mean that I don't love him and trust him."

"Violence and romance." Grinning thinly, Jake turned to face her. "Tell me—what happened to Globo?"

"He's in a cell down below. I want to look into his case myself."

"While I was in Cuidado, Globo arranged to have me knocked off."

"Yet you took a risk like tonight's to save his life?"

"Hell, he was going to be executed for the wrong thing—that's not justice," he told her. "After Globo's plan to get rid of me went flooey, I had a nice chat with him. He says it was Vargas who hired him for the job."

She stood. "That seems unlikely, since Rafe didn't even know you were in Mexico."

"Sure, he did. Globo contacted him—or somebody close to him. I told you, I've been trying to arrange a meeting with you."

"Then are you suggesting that Rafe is jealous of you—that he doesn't want an old lover of mine turning up again?"

"Nope, that's not Vargas' reason at all."

"Then what is?"

"Quite a few people are interested in Kittridge. That's because he's come up with a way to render just about every Tek chip on the face of the Earth absolutely useless," Jake said. "If I find him first, then that process'll be used to wipe out the Tek trade. For a while anyway."

"You're claiming that Rafe wants to keep you from locating the professor?"

"Yeah. And I'm pretty certain he knows where Kittridge and his daughter are."

Angry lines appeared on her forehead and around her mouth. "I don't see what your reason is for trying to turn me against him."

"Propaganda and persuasion isn't my specialty, Elana," he said. "But I intend to find the Kittridges—and I figure Rafe Vargas is one of those who's trying to stop me."

Very slowly Warbride said, "If that's true—then it means he's lying to me, keeping back the truth."

"It also means he's tied in with the Tek trade."

Her metal fingers tightened into a fist. "We have nothing to do with Tek, Jake, not a damn thing," she told him. "You must know how I feel about that stuff—especially because of my brother."

"Most of the recent rulers of your country haven't exactly shared your views."

She hit the palm of her flesh hand with her metal fist. "If I collaborate with the Tek lords then I'm no better than that *puta,* President Romero."

"And Vargas agrees with you?"

After a few seconds she replied, "I've been assuming that he does, yes." She took several striding steps toward the door, turned and pointed at him with her metal forefinger. "Come along, Jake, we'll settle all this right now."

Saying nothing, he followed Warbride out of the room.

*

The light from the overhead globes made the metal side of Vargas' face glow palely silver. He was still in his uniform, and the medals on his broad chest glowed, too. He was sitting in a lucite armchair near the center of his room. When Warbride came striding in, the portion of his mouth that showed broke into a smile. "I want you to know, *cara,* that I completely forgive you for—". Then he saw Jake. "Why did you bring this *cabrón* here?"

Warbride halted a few feet from his chair. "We want to discuss something with you, Rafe."

"We?" He was watching Jake. "Since when do you allow *gringos* to—"

"I want to know," she demanded, putting hands on hips, "if you had anything to do with plans to have Jake killed."

Vargas brought his silver fingers up to touch at his silver cheek. "Has he come whining to you with some childish fairy tale of—"

"Vargas," cut in Jake, "I used to know her pretty well. I don't think evasive bullshit is going to work."

"You allow this man—fresh out of jail—to come here and accuse me?"

"Did you?" she asked.

"What possible reason would—"

"I can have Globo brought here."

Vargas stood up, turning his back to both of them. "Very well, but you're going to be angry with me, *chiquita,*" he predicted. "Keep in mind, though, how much I love you, and how much you mean to me. When I heard that Jake Cardigan wanted to come here for—"

"Why wasn't I told about that?"

Back still to her, Vargas held out his metal hand and made a be-patient gesture. "I was—forgive me, it was childish—but I was jealous. I knew that you two had once been very close—granted it was many years ago—and I simply didn't want him seeing you again."

"That was a decision I should have made, Rafe."

"Yes, surely," admitted Vargas, shoulders slumping slightly. "It was wrong, *cara,* as was my foolish plan to have this insignificant *cucaracha* killed. Once I saw him face to face—why, I realized he was nothing but a pathetic, burned-out failure. Certainly no competition for me."

Warbride asked him, "What about Kittridge?"

"Who?"

"Kittridge," she repeated.

"I'm afraid, *bonita,* that I don't know the professor."

"Yet you're aware he's a professor?"

"Perhaps I've heard of him somewhere. A *gringo,* is he not?"

Reaching out with her metal hand, Warbride caught his shoulder and turned him around so he was facing her again. "Look in my eyes, Rafe," she ordered. "Do you know anything about the crash of a skycruiser—Kittridge's skycruiser—near here?"

He shook his head, but his eyes were on the lightglobe floating a few feet above his head. "Nothing, *cara,* except that it crashed."

"Rafe!" She put her metal hand to one side of his head, her flesh hand to the other, and forced him to meet her gaze. "Swear to me that you—"

"I don't have to swear a damn thing." He pulled free, backed away from her. "Either you trust me or you don't."

"At the moment I have doubts," Warbride admitted. "Again I ask you—what do you know of the crash?"

Vargas went over to the far side of the room to stand looking out a window. "There was no crash," he said finally. "That was only a story that was circulated."

"Then what did happen?"

Vargas watched the night wind worrying the treetops. "Keep in mind that funds for our cause are not always that easy to come by, *cara,* despite our many recent victories."

"You made some sort of deal?"

"The skycruiser was forced down in the *Selva Grande,*" he answered. "For not interfering with that operation, for providing certain people safe conduct—well, we added a considerable sum to our treasury."

Jake asked him, "Who paid you the money?"

Vargas didn't respond.

Warbride said, "Answer, Rafe. I, too, am interested."

"As I understand it, though I never met him directly—the money came from Sonny Hokori."

"*Mierda.* You've been dealing with the Tek people while—"

"This has nothing to do with selling Tek, or even with manufacturing it. Hokori wanted to waylay Kittridge and his daughter, and he was willing to pay well for our cooperation. His people took care of all the details."

Jake eased closer to him. "What did they do with the Kittridges after the cruiser was forced down?"

"I don't know."

"But they weren't killed?"

"Not to my knowledge."

"Where were they taken?"

"I also have no knowledge of that."

"What about Sonny Hokori—where's he?"

"As of two days ago Hokori was in Acapulco. At the Pleasure Dome, his casino complex there."

"Could Kittridge and his daughter have been taken there?"

"It's possible, but I don't know."

Jake next asked, "What about Bennett Sands?"

"He wasn't involved in any of this—if that's what you want to know."

Warbride asked, "How much did Hokori pay you?"

Vargas looked back over his shoulder at her. "He paid us a handsome sum."

"Specifically?"

"It was—it was five hundred thousand dollars in American dollars, *chiquita.*"

"Where is that money?"

Vargas looked up at another of the floating globes of light. "As a matter of fact, it's still here in my quarters. I was intending to turn it over to you—and to explain all that had happened. But then this *gringo* intruded on us and—"

"Rafe," she said, "this is *muy triste.*"

He touched his silver fingers to his silver cheek again. "But we've cleared the air now, been honest with each other—although I must admit I would have preferred to have this little talk in private and without a hostile intruder taking it all in."

"I have loved you, Rafe," she said sadly. "But you're of no use to me if I can't trust you."

"But you can trust me, *cara.* Haven't I told you everything?"

Warbride shook her head. "But too late, much too late." Her metal arm swung up and her middle finger pointed at him.

"No, *cara*—please . . ."

An intense beam of crimson light went leaping from her fingertip.

It hit Vargas in the chest as he was trying to back away. Medals and ribbons burned and melted first and then a small, neat hole was burned clean through him. Blood came pumping out of the hole and then out of what showed of his mouth. Vargas' arms flapped and he fell back against the wall. He stayed there until he died, which only took five seconds.

"Jesus, Warbride . . ." said Jake.

"I'm glad to see," she said with a satisfied smile, "that you're finally calling me by my right name."

The dawn was gray and chill. Beth didn't say anything as Jake guided the borrowed black skycruiser up above the clearing. When they were hovering over the highest treetops, he punched out a flight pattern for Acapulco.

"Why so glum?" he asked, relaxing in the pilot seat as the cruiser started cutting through the beginning day. "You miss Ogden Swires?"

She had been looking straight ahead and continued to do so. "I suppose I ought to apologize for the way I'm feeling," she said. "Except I can't control the emotions that've been built into me."

"Which emotion is producing that scowl?"

"I'd like to ask you something, Jake."

"Go ahead."

"Did you spend the night with that wild woman?"

"Only part of it."

"Well, I suppose that was to be expected, since years ago you and she were—"

"Whoa—I didn't spend the time in bed," Jake told her. "I was getting information."

She turned to look at him. "What did you find out?"

"The crash was faked," he answered, "with Vargas' help."

She pressed her hands together. "They're alive?"

"They should be."

"Where—in Acapulco?"

"We'll start looking there, since that's where Sonny Hokori is supposed to be."

"Then Hokori is the one behind what's going on?"

"He's behind what happened to your father."

She laughed quietly. "To Beth and her father, you mean."

Nodding, he said, "Kittridge and Beth were forced down near Warbride's encampment. Since Hokori's involved, it's likely he had them brought to him."

"That would be to the Pleasure Dome, wouldn't it?"

"Yeah. Ever been there?"

"No, but it was a favorite spot of Bennett Sands, and he talked about it," she said. "Did Vargas say anything about him?"

"Only that Sands isn't tied in."

Beth looked out at the Great Forest beneath them. "Why did Vargas confide all this in you? The last time I saw you two together, you weren't exactly—"

"Warbride mentioned that you weren't too happy with what she did—and told her so. I appreciate your support, Beth, but that was risky."

"My temper sometimes overcomes my reason. Now tell me about General Vargas and why he decided to confide in you."

"I had Warbride along—she did most of the questioning."

"Didn't she know about the skycruiser being forced down?"

"Apparently not."

"And you believe her?"

"She was very convincing," he said. "After she found out what Vargas had been up to—she killed him."

"Jake." Beth put her hand on his arm. "I thought they were lovers."

"They were, sure. But she won't allow anybody, not even a lover, to make deals she doesn't know about."

"She might have killed you, too."

Jake grinned. "No, because she trusts me."

"Sometimes I wish . . ."

"Wish what?"

"Oh, it's only that all of this, people killing each other and trying to kill us—I just wish it were over."

"Ought to be fairly soon."

"Last night I was thinking about something I did when I was eighteen," Beth confided. "Everything had been getting too much for me—school, romance and my father. Being a very affluent and fairly spoiled kid, I ran away to the Moon."

"That's impressive. I took off once when I was nine, but I only got as far as the Glendale Sector. How long before they found you?"

"Almost a week. I'd just been hiding out at a villa my uncle has up there. It's way out in the Old Settlement area and he rarely visits it himself, but he feels good knowing the place is there should he decide to hop up there for a lunar vacation. It's all staffed by robots—and some very old and antiquated robots they are."

"The place is still there?"

"Yes. I was even thinking last night that I'd like to head for there again," she admitted. "Except a couple of things keep me here. I want to find my father and—well, I'd like to stay with you as long as I can."

After a few silent seconds Jake said, "I'm glad you didn't run away."

She smiled and leaned back in her seat. "I still remember the keyword for getting into the place and activating my uncle's villa. It's *eclectic.*"

"Eclectic's not a very dramatic keyword."

"My uncle sees the universe as basically eclectic." Reaching out, she took hold of Jake's hand. "I thought for a few minutes there last night, you know, that Warbride had killed you."

"So did I."

"And for those few minutes I really felt as though I'd lost something important."

After a while Jake moved his hand free of hers.

The Acapulco Ritz had five tapfree vidphones on its mezzanine floor. After Jake and Beth checked into a suite high in Tower 3, he went down to use one of the phones.

A gold-plated robot with a permanent smile greeted him in three languages and escorted him into a bugproof phoneroom.

Seated in front of the phonescreen, Jake put through a call to the Cosmos Detective Agency in GLA.

A lovely crimson-haired young woman appeared on the screen. "Cosmos Detec . . . Yikes!"

"How's that again?"

"It is you, isn't it, Jake?"

"It is. Are you Marny?"

She fluffed her hair. "I abandoned my andy look," the agency receptionist explained. "But the important thing is—we'd heard you'd maybe been bumped off down there in Mexico. Trampled by wild bulls was one rumor, gunned down by a jealous rival of Warbride's was another."

"Some truth in both rumors," he acknowledged. "But I'm still above the ground. I want to report in, and find out how Gomez is doing."

"You can talk to him."

"He's in the office?"

"Against his medics' orders. Hobbling around in a most pathetic, but sort of sexy, way."

"Put him on, Marny, please."

"Surely. And, oh, do you think I look less mechanical this way?"

"Much less."

She smiled, the screen blanked for eight seconds and then Gomez appeared.

He was seated at a desk with a smudged stretch of afternoon sky showing out the high, thin window behind him. "*Amigo,*" he said, smiling. "I'm very please to note that you're not defunct."

"Not completely as yet. How are you?"

"Doing as well as can be expected. A plascast on one's leg, by the way, brings out the maternal in all sorts and conditions of women," said his partner. "Where are you?"

"Acapulco," answered Jake. "Listen, I'm a little wary about my old contacts down here. Do you have somebody trustworthy you can suggest?"

"Who you going up against? Sonny Hokori and associates?"

"For a start, yes."

"Be very cautious, *amigo,*" advised Gomez. "Let's see—you can try Carmelita Jimenez at the Dalton-Walden American Faxbook Centre. Don't let her demure demeanor fool you. For general information see Gutierrez at the Club Latino. How are you progressing with the case?"

"It could be that Kittridge and his daughter are here."

"What leads you to that conclusion?"

Jake, concisely, gave Gomez an account of what he'd been up to since arriving across the border.

When Jake concluded, Gomez looked up from the notes he'd been taking. "This android rep of Beth Kittridge . . ." he said.

"What about her?"

"You're holding something back, aren't you? I don't know, there's something that comes into your voice when you talk about her."

"You and I have been partners too long. It's tough to hide anything from you," said Jake. "Well, what seems to be happening—hell, I'm getting fond of Beth."

"Except that this isn't really Beth."

"Exactly, yeah. But in a way she is."

"I had a crush on a hologram stripper when I was sixteen."

"I suppose that's about what this sounds like."

"No, actually it's a tricky situation, *amigo.*"

"What I'm certain of is that I want to find Beth Kittridge alive," said Jake. "And not only because I was hired to locate her."

Gomez, with too much attention to detail, shut his notebook and moved it to the side of his desk. "Listen, Jake, I think I better mention this," he said. "Kate is trying to get in touch with you. Somehow she's found out that you're down there in Mexico, and she says she has to talk to you. That it's—"

"Something happened to my son?"

"I don't believe so, *amigo,* but the lady didn't give me any details. She says it's urgent."

"I better call her."

"She informs me she's not at home and moving about a lot, so she wants to have a number where she can contact you. She's been calling the office every couple hours since yesterday."

"How'd she know I was working for Cosmos?"

"I'm not sure she did. But she was aware that I am gainfully employed here. Since I am your long-time bosom chum, she assumed I'd know how to reach you."

"Okay, you can tell her to call me here at the Acapulco Ritz."

"Is that safe to do?"

"She's my wife—she used to be my wife. Yeah, you can let her know I'm here."

"I'll do that."

"Keep on recuperating, Sid."

"You, too," said Gomez.

Stretching away in every direction were the endless rows of tall towers and skyscrapers, each of the multistory plasglass, metal and stone buildings linked with pedramps and walkways at various levels. A thin mist was drifting in from the sea as twilight began to spread across Acapulco. Countless lights, of every color, were coming to life.

"Looks like a combination of the Borderland and the *Selva Grande,*" remarked Jake, turning away from the tinted wraparound window of their suite's living room.

Beth asked him, "Isn't it something you've been anxious to do?"

"Talk to Kate, you mean?"

"I thought that was one of the reasons you took this job, so you'd be able to look her up while you were in Mexico."

"Let's just say," he said, sitting in a black armchair that faced the black sofa she was occupying, "I have mixed feelings."

"Why exactly did you separate?"

"The State of Southern California arranged that."

"She divorced you while you were in the Freezer?"

"Yeah. That's a fairly common occurrence with guys who're in prison," he said. "Especially when you get sent up to the Freezer. It's a little closer to being dead, and some wives get very uneasy."

"Even so, you didn't expect a divorce?"

"Nope." He leaned back in his big, soft chair, didn't feel especially comfortable, sat up straight again. "Actually Kate had left me once before, back about six years ago."

"Why?"

He became interested in the palm of his left hand, started rubbing at it with the fingers of his right. "Being a cop's wife can be rough. I'd been working on an investigation of one of the top suspected Tek distributors in Greater Los Angeles—and, from what Kate told me later, there'd been some threats made against her and Dan."

"She didn't tell you at the time?"

"She was like that, kept things to herself. She simply decided that it would be better if she went to live in New England with some relatives of hers. She put Dan in a private school, supposedly a very good one, in Boston."

"That's not as bad as going to the Sky Academy."

"I'd never wanted to send him away to any school, by himself and away from me. That was mostly because—"

"You were trying hard not to be like your father."

"That was it, yeah. But Dan ended up going through something like that anyway."

"What about Kate's job?"

"Sands had just opened a branch in Rhode Island and she was able to work there."

"That must've been about the same time Sands was in New England himself, looking after the plant opening."

"The reason Kate left GLA was because of the threats, not because of Sands," he told Beth. "When people talk about Tek wars, they assume that just means what happens between rival dealers and manufacturers. But almost everybody gets involved, cops included, and sometimes there can be unanticipated casualties."

"The investigation you were working on when she left you—is that the one that was dropped?"

"Yeah, the one that was dropped, the one they said I used my influence to get sidetracked," Jake answered. "The fact that I had nothing to do with the investigation's being stopped wasn't believed by too many people. That's why I ended up in the Freezer."

"Your wife believed in you, though?"

"She and Dan both. They had come back before that—just a few months before I got arrested."

"You were also charged with being a Tek user."

Twilight was closing in outside; the room was turning dusky.

Jake nodded slowly. "That part was true," he admitted. "Fact is,

I started using the stuff the night I came home and found my wife and son had left. I made use of a Brainbox and a Tek chip I was keeping as evidence in another case."

"Once in college I tried Tek," she said, "but I didn't find it that satisfying."

"Maybe it depends on what kind of illusions you use Tek for," he said. "I just used it to relive the past, and improve it a lot, and to spruce up the present. In my Tek world my father and I got along fine, my mother was still alive, Kate never left me and I wasn't hooked on Tek." He stood up. "Time to go look up Gomez's contacts. If Kate calls—find out where I can reach her."

"You sure you don't want me to come along?"

"Not on this initial run, no." Crossing to her, he bent and kissed her on the cheek. "Stay here, Beth, and be watchful."

Jake strode a pedramp twenty stories above the ground level. The ramp was wide and had chest-high guard walls of tinted plasglass running along each side. Small globes of colored light dotted the top of each wall at intervals of three feet, red, yellow and blue, continually blinking.

In the sky high above, a huge skyvan was slowly gliding through the misty twilight. A giant vidscreen was imbedded in its underbelly, showing images of President Romero.

"Not a fetching woman," Jake said to himself.

A group of tourists came spilling out of an indoor park up ahead.

"Don't go so close to the edge, Leroy."

"It's perfectly safe, Mom. They got a wall."

"Those look awfully flimsy to me."

"That's because you have vertigo."

Weaving his way deftly through this newest batch of pedestrians, Jake continued.

The Dalton-Walden American Faxbook Centre had a blank, off-white front. Beneath its name, which was discreetly lettered in neon next to the door, ran a small line of copy—ALL THE LATEST BESTSELLERS FROM THE UNITED STATES.

As Jake neared the off-white door, it hissed open. There were six faxbook printers around the circular, blank-walled room. The store's only customer was seated in front of the small, gray printer nearest the entryway.

Scowling, he was thrusting his Banx card into the proper slot. He then typed out the title of the book he wanted and eyed the machine warily. He was middle-sized and middle-aged, a few pounds overweight and nearly bald.

"Not available either, sir," said the voxbox of the printer.

"It's a bestseller, isn't it?"

"Yes, sir."

"It's on sale in America, isn't it?"

"Yes, sir."

"This shop allegedly sells copies of American bestsellers. I want it."

"This particular bestseller, sir, is unfortunately on the Unacceptable list here in Mexico."

"You're telling me I can't buy a copy?"

"I am, sir."

"Okay, okay. There's one more I want." He tried another title on the keyboard.

"That one is available."

"Good—print me a copy of the damn thing."

"You must first, sir, go obtain a permit from the office of the Bishop of Acapulco before you can purchase it."

The customer yanked his Banx card free of the faxbook printer, shoved back his chair. "Let me tell you what I think of freedom of the press here in Mexico."

"Before you do, sir, allow me to remind you that we have your name and hotel address on record."

The man reflected for about five seconds. He slipped his Banx card away, frowned at Jake, stomped out of the bookstore.

Jake glanced at the desk at the room's middle. There was no one behind it. He crossed to the only other door and tapped on it.

"If the printer won't print it, there's nothing I can do," called a woman's voice from the other side of the door.

"Carmelita?"

"*Sí.*"

"Jake Cardigan."

The door slid open and a plump, dark-haired woman of forty stood smiling out at him. "Gomez phoned me about you." After shaking hands, she beckoned him to come into the small back room.

"Exactly how many different books can anybody buy in your store?" he asked, taking one of the two chairs.

"The list is down to seven. President Romero isn't especially open-minded." She sat in the other chair. "This room's bugproof."

Jake rested a hand on his knee. "The Pleasure Dome."

"A dangerous place for an American detective."

"Is Sonny Hokori there now?"

"*Sí,*" replied Carmelita. "He's been back nearly two weeks."

"He has living quarters inside?"

"He does, very lavish ones."

"What about Professor Kittridge and his daughter—are they inside the Pleasure Dome?"

"Gomez asked me that. But I don't know," she said. "I can, very discreetly, try to find out."

"If they are, I have to get inside."

"More importantly, you have to get out again."

"Right. Bringing them with me."

Carmelita laughed. "You've got even more self-confidence than that bastard Gomez."

"Can it be done?"

"I'll need at least a day to find out. Do you have that much time, Jake?"

"Maybe, but not much more," he answered. "Is Bennett Sands in Acapulco?"

"He arrived shortly after Sonny Hokori."

"Are the two of them tied together?"

"A safe bet, though I have no proof."

"Can you get any?"

"Not in a day, not if I'm going to arrange sneaking you in and out of the Dome."

Jake got up. "Can I contact you anyplace besides here?"

"It's safer to let me do the contacting," she told him. "Gomez got himself hurt—is it serious? He wouldn't tell me."

"A broken leg."

"That won't bother him much."

"It won't," agreed Jake and took his leave.

There she was, up ahead in the mist, a faint sad smile touching her pretty face. And for a moment Jake lost four years.

But as he moved across the wide pedramp to the shadowy doorway where she stood waiting, he returned to the present. He saw that she was thinner, and the weary look he'd noticed on the vidphone call still haunted her face. And there was something different about her, reflecting all the things that had happened to her that had nothing to do with him.

Very quietly Jake said, "This is a surprise, Kate."

"I have to talk to you."

He halted two feet from her, not reaching out to touch her. "Is it Dan—is he all right?"

"Yes, he's fine." Very cautiously she took hold of his arm. "There's a little hologram park near here. We can talk there. I don't have much time, Jake."

Walking at his former wife's side, he asked, "Where's Dan, with you or—"

"Dan is fine, really. He's going to a private school in Mexico City. This has nothing to do with him."

Kate glanced around nervously while Jake paid the sombreroed robot at the gateway of the indoor park.

"How'd you get to Acapulco so fast, Kate? Gomez couldn't have told you where I was more than a few—"

"I was already here." She hurried along a grassy path that wound its way through a believable stretch of dense jungle. "You have to listen to me—I only have a few minutes."

"Have you been sick?"

She touched at her short hair. "I've lost some weight, that's all," she said, stopping at a wrought-iron bench and sitting. "And, hell—

I'm almost five years older than I was when you saw me last. You look great, by the way."

"Sure." He sat on the bench, not too close to her. "Okay, tell me what's going on, Kate."

"Listen—you must get out of Acapulco. You and that girl. Right now, Jake—right away."

Bright jungle birds seemed to be flying up above the projected branches of the tall trees.

"Why?"

"I don't have all the details, which is maybe just as well. I do know they mean to kill you."

"Who's doing the job?"

She brushed at her auburn hair again. "Some people—some dangerous people who work for Sonny Hokori."

"How do you know?"

"It doesn't matter. I just know. Trust me, Jake, and get the hell out of town, get back to GLA fast as you can."

"It *does* matter how you found out, Kate." He took hold of her hand, and there was no affection in his touch. "Did you overhear a conversation at a party? Catch a mention on the news—what?"

She sighed. "Still a cop, no matter what they did to you," she said, pulling her hand free. "Keep hitting at the suspect, badger the truth out no matter what the—"

"Who's planning to kill me—and how do you know it, Kate?"

"Damn it—you must know I'm involved with Bennett again."

"Again?"

"You knew about the other time, didn't you?" she said. "In Greater Los Angeles, while we were still married and I was working for him. It was right before your . . . trouble."

"My trouble . . . yeah," he said slowly. "And what did Bennett Sands have to do with my trouble?"

Kate inhaled sharply. "Nothing," she said. "I'm . . . Yes, I'm certain of that."

"But now—here and now—Sands is in cahoots with Hokori, isn't he?"

"Yes, he seems to be," she answered, her voice low. "But, Jake, honestly, I only found out about it just recently. Believe me."

"Back then, during our happy married days—back when I was

supposed to be aware that you were sleeping with him—did you ever happen to confide in Sands about the cases I was working on, about whom I was investigating?"

"I may have. We talked about all sorts of things, because Bennett always had time to listen to me. You were such a bright cop—one of the best in GLA they said. So I figured, really, Jake, you'd be able to figure out who your wife was fooling around with."

Jake sat back on the bench, looking up at the trees. "Tek," he said finally.

"What?"

"Everything is just Tek, just illusions. I always thought that you—hell, never mind."

"I overheard Bennett talking to some of Sonny Hokori's people," she said, standing. "They knew you'd be coming here to Acapulco and they want you dead. Get away—please!"

He stood up. "What about the Kittridges?"

"I don't know anything about them," she swore. "I just couldn't let anyone kill you."

"Nope—you couldn't do that."

"I have to go." She turned and walked away from him.

Jake made no attempt to follow her.

The mist had grown thick and it was pressing against the windows of the living room of their suite. The night city looked fragmented. Parts of it were blurred, parts lost completely in the gray fog. High on the side of a government tower across the way, a two-story vidnews screen seemed to be floating. Silent images of the funeral of a public official showed on the huge screen. A black skyhearse circling a sun-bright slanting hillside cemetery, six ebony robots carrying a black coffin, a gaunt old woman, sobbing, being supported and comforted by a gleaming silvery priestbot.

Jake turned away from the misty view. "No, not exactly," he said in answer to a question Beth had asked him nearly a minute earlier. "I was angry mostly. Sad, too."

"But not happy, not glad to see Kate again?" Beth was sitting on the shadowy side of the room, surrounded by darkness.

"I guess that in the time since I left the Freezer," he said, "I've changed some. I'm finally starting to wake up."

"Everything she told you, Jake, may be the absolute truth."

"Sure, I don't doubt Sands is a partner of Sonny Hokori's. Nor that they're all anxious to kill me."

"I meant the part about your wife's not knowing whether Bennett—"

"Former wife," he corrected.

"Not knowing if Sands was involved in framing you four years back."

"I'm betting he was."

"Even if that's so, it doesn't mean Kate had anything to do with setting you up. She may just have told him more than she should have about the Tek cases you were working on."

"Just bedside conversation, huh?"

"What bothers you most, Jake—that she slept with him or that she told him about your police work?"

He looked again out at the night. The funeral was over, replaced by a parade along a rain-swept street in Mexico City. "Both," he replied. "No, wait. What really unsettles me is the way Kate talked about our marriage. There was such a bitterness in her voice, such . . . Hell, none of this has anything to do with the job at hand."

"From what you said earlier—you're pretty certain Hokori has my father at the Pleasure Dome," Beth said from the shadows.

"I figured that as a strong possibility, even before I talked to Carmelita."

"If you confirm it—then why not contact your agency for some assistance?"

Jake grinned at her. "Have them send two or three husky bodyguards?"

"A half dozen or so first-rate operatives to assist you in raiding the Dome. Going up against Hokori and his bunch all by yourself, which is what you sound like you're planning to do, is a shade on the dumb side, Jake."

"Waiting around until Cosmos ships me a crew would—"

The vidphone buzzed.

Jake crossed over and answered it. "Yeah?"

Carmen Jimenez was on the screen. "Señor Cardigan, please."

"That's me."

"I'm calling from the Dalton-Walden shop, Señor Cardigan," the plump woman said in a businesslike way. "The book you ordered this afternoon has just come off the printer. I know you're most anxious to read it, so if you'd like to drop in at the shop I'll keep open until you arrive."

"Yes. That's very nice of you. Fifteen minutes." He hung up.

"Meaning she's got some information for you?"

"Yeah," said Jake, "so I'll head for—"

"We'll head for the store."

"I'd rather you—"

"No, I'll feel better if I tag along." Beth stood, still in the shadows. "It's only a short way—we can use the pedramps."

After a few seconds he said, "Sure, come along."

The heavy night fog came swirling over the plasglass safety walls, spilling down onto the ribbed surface of the pedramp, tangling with legs and feet. The lights along the tops of the chest-high walls made small, fuzzy splotches of blinking light in the thick gray mist.

Beth had an arm linked with his. "I think we're passing," she informed him.

"Hum?"

"I was saying that I believe we're being accepted by all of these milling pedestrians as just another tourist couple."

"Father and daughter on vacation?"

Laughing, Beth said, "More likely newlyweds on their honeymoon."

Jake grinned. "Sorry, I wasn't paying attention a minute ago."

"Brooding, were you?"

"In a way," he admitted, moving closer to her to avoid a wobbling group of American skysailors who'd just come charging, most of them laughing and shouting, out of a mechanical *cantina.* "I was thinking about Kate, wondering why I never tumbled to what was going on. A wife having an affair with her boss is a pretty frequent thing, a domestic-life cliché, yet I missed almost every damn clue."

"You can't always be a cop or a detective in your own home."

"That's sure what Kate feels I was. Actually, though, I was as dense as—"

"It's very tough, isn't it, for you to admit you're not perfect?"

Six school kids, escorted by a robot nanny whose solid gunmetal legs were pumping hard to keep up with her charges, came running by from the opposite direction.

"Sure, I can accept not being perfect. But behaving like a lovestruck teenager with Kate is harder to accommodate."

"Sometime," she said, her hold on his arm tightening, "we'll have to compare notes on our fathers—and the effect they've had on our lives."

"My impression is that you and the professor have an ideal—"

"Not quite, Jake. In some ways he's as tough and unbending as I imagine your military dad was," she said. "And I'm not always sure lately that—well, that he's being truthful and straightforward with me."

"Because of the trip to Mexico?"

"What's really exasperating is the fact that my memory cuts off several days before the actual trip," she said. "I've had the feeling, for the past day or more, that I was on the brink of finding out something—something important."

"Such as the fact that your father and Sands had made some sort of deal that you weren't in on?"

"That's yes, one possibility," admitted Beth with an affirmative nod. "We learned from Warbride—you did actually—that there never was actually any crash. It was faked. I'm wondering, really, if my father might have known in advance."

"That would mean he was definitely planning to sell out to Sonny Hokori," said Jake. "But you should've gotten some hint of that."

"Perhaps I did. Especially during those final days that are missing from my memory."

"Still and all, Beth, it might be better to assume that he . . ." Jake stopped talking, stopped walking.

About a hundred yards ahead of them a tall, slim boy of about fourteen was standing near a restbench and looking anxiously their way. He had hair just a few shades darker than Jake's, a grin that was a younger and much less cynical version of Jake's.

Beth saw that Jake was staring at the boy. "What's wrong?"

"It's got to be him—it's Dan." He waved, laughing, hand high in the foggy air.

The boy's grin widened as he returned the wave. He started pushing his way through the people on the pedramp.

"Wait, Jake," cautioned Beth, eyes narrowing. She caught hold of his arm.

"It's my son, Beth." Jerking free of her, he started running.

The boy was running, too, dodging through the crowd. "Dad!"

"No, don't." Sprinting, Beth caught up with Jake. She gave him a sudden, rough shove.

He stumbled to his left, fell to one knee. A fat tourist decked with cameras tripped over him and they became entangled.

Beth kept running. It was she who met the boy.

He tried to avoid her, his face growing dark with anger.

But she threw both arms tight around him. They went staggering against the nearest plasglass wall.

The wall cracked; a whole jagged section broke free under their combined weight.

An old man screamed and brought both gnarled hands up to mask his weathered face; a young skysailor cried out and made a grab for Beth and the boy she was hugging. He missed, catching only air.

Beth and the boy went falling over the edge of the ramp. Locked together, they plummeted down through the swirling gray fog, falling toward the thousands of blurred lights far below.

Jake had gotten to his feet, gone stumbling and shoving to the gap torn in the guardwall.

"Why, Beth?" he muttered.

Then came the explosion, while the two of them were still dropping.

A great harsh flowering of intense red and yellow flame that ripped through the fog. Snarls of harsh black smoke spilling across the gray night.

The remains of the two of them went flying and spinning, scattered forever. Twists of metal and plastic, shards of glass, unraveling ribbons of bright-colored wire.

All the fragments and tatters drifted down and away and were swallowed by the fog. Silence seemed to spread across the ramp; for a moment there didn't seem to be a sound in the entire city.

"He wasn't Dan, he was a kamikaze android sent to kill me," Jake said to himself. "Beth sensed that."

Staring down and down at nothing, he started to cry.

After a while Jake wandered down to the ground level of Acapulco. He thought at first that he wasn't looking for anything at all, and then for a while he thought he was hunting for Tek.

Because once he got hold of a Brainbox and hooked himself up to it, he could relive the past few hours. On the second go-round, though, Beth wouldn't die.

And maybe the kamikaze android would actually be Dan. His son would've run away from his private school up in Mexico City to be here with Jake.

There wouldn't be anyplace for Kate in the Tek fantasy Jake was going to have.

"Help me buy a leg, *señor.*" A one-legged beggar was perched on a crate that had once, according to the legend on its side, held WELFARE FOOD/COURTESY SANDS INDUSTRIES.

"How much do you still need?"

"Only thirteen hundred dollars American."

Jake gave him a $10 note. "How long have you been collecting for it?"

"It will be, *señor,* seven years this next Christmas. *Gracias* for your small contribution."

"De nada."

Jake turned onto a narrow, ground-level street that smelled richly of neglected garbage.

"I got what you want, *señor.*"

"Which is?"

The robot was covered with rainbow designs that had been painted on his dented gunmetal body with thick glopaint. "I got ladies, *señor.* Young ones, even a few mature ones," explained the mechanical man.

"Where can I get some Tek?"

"Aw, *señor,*" said the robot pimp disdainfully. "I'm not selling illusions and escapes from reality here. Don't let my format fool you. No, I manage only live talent. Real *mujeres,* not fantasy ones."

Shaking his head, Jake moved along.

But in front of a burned-out *cantina* he halted. "If it's obvious to a robot pimp," he said to himself, "it ought to be obvious to me. Yeah, I don't think after all I want to escape from reality just yet. There are a few things to take care of first."

He started back for the upper levels of the city.

Kate, as always, slept naked. She awakened when the overhead lights in the big bedroom blossomed. She sat up in the wide oval bed and stared at him, making no effort to pull up the sheet.

Jake gave a negative shake of his head as she started to speak. He drew a wooden chair over close beside the opposite side of the bed, picked up the snub-nosed lazgun off the night table and then seated himself in the chair.

With the barrel of the gun he reached out to nudge the still sleeping Bennett Sands in the ribs.

Sands murmured negatively, sighed, turned away from Jake.

Jake prodded him again, this time in the region of his kidneys.

Stiffening, Sands rolled over on his back and opened his eyes. Then he tried to rise, reaching out toward where his lazgun was supposed to be.

"Not there," mentioned Jake, showing the weapon to him.

Sands's face was pale and puffy; his eyes underscored with shadowy patches of skin. "How the hell did you get in here, Cardigan?" Pushing with his elbows, thrashing some, he grunted himself into a sitting position. His candy-striped nightshirt was wrinkled, twisted on his lean body. "I've got one of the best available secsystems in this damn villa and I—"

"I'm pretty handy at circumventing security setups," Jake explained to him. "And just to be on the safe side, I brought along a highly efficient tech housebreaker and three ordinary burglars. It helped that I was also able to bribe most of your servants."

"Jake," said Kate, "it wasn't very smart of you to—"

"I'll handle this, Katie," Sands told her without taking his eyes off Jake. "Cardigan, you can't just break into my villa this way. That violates all sorts of laws and—"

"I haven't been a cop for a long time," he reminded him. "Besides, this is Mexico."

"It is, Cardigan, and it would do you well to keep in mind that I have considerable influence in this country. You've put yourself in—"

"Get up now, would you . . ."

"I'm going to make considerable trouble for you, not only with the local law but—"

"In order to do that, you'd have to be alive," Jake pointed out. "And unless you start cooperating, you may not continue to be. Up—start dressing. We have someplace to go."

"Jake, it would be really very foolish to kill Bennett. I realize you're terribly jealous, but—"

"Jealousy doesn't have a damn thing to do with this," he assured his former wife. "Sands—get moving!"

Swinging, slowly, out of the big bed, Sands asked, "Where exactly do you fancy we're going together, Cardigan?"

"To the Pleasure Dome for a chat with Sonny Hokori."

Sands's red and white nightshirt fluttered when he gave a thin, nasal laugh. "You can't really be serious? Sonny will simply destroy you should you venture anywhere near him."

"Better hope he doesn't, because you'll go, too," said Jake. "It'll be a good idea if you see to it that I stay alive during our visit to the Dome."

"This kind of thoughtless bravado is exactly what got you in trouble in GLA."

"Yeah, that and some help from you and Sonny," amended Jake. "Now get yourself into some clothes, Sands—I'm not especially patient tonight."

"We could remain right here," suggested Sands, "and discuss whatever it is you think you have to say to Sonny."

"Dress," advised Jake. "I'd prefer to use you to get me into the place. It's simpler, but it's not the only way."

"All right, Cardigan, very well. But you're being very unwise, extremely so."

From the bed Kate asked, "Jake, did anyone—has anyone—tried to hurt you?"

"Yeah," he answered, "but they didn't succeed."

"Not so far," said Sands.

The robot was tall. It stood a good seven feet in height, and one of the small squares of red plasglass implanted in its white-enameled chest had begun flashing. With a shuffling step, it moved to block Entrance B to the Pleasure Dome.

"No weapons allowed inside, gentlemen," the guardbot told Jake and Sands while they were still climbing the broad white stairway to the arched entrance to the great white dome.

"Too bad, Cardigan, but it looks like you won't be able to get any closer than Sonny's doorstep." Sands halted two steps below the robot guard.

"If you'll just hand over your gun, sir, it will be returned to you when you depart from the Pleasure Dome."

Jake was just behind the other man, a spare jacket he'd borrowed from the bedroom closet at the villa draped over his arm and hand, concealing the lazgun. He jabbed at Sands's back with the barrel. "Override the robot," he instructed quietly.

"I'm afraid I don't quite understand what you're—"

"You and Sonny's other henchmen come and go all the time carrying weapons. So give this guard the password."

"Why should I help you to—"

"I wasn't kidding about having no more patience tonight. Do it, do it now or I'll drop you right here."

After running his tongue over his lips, Sands nodded up at the robot and said, *"Nijuu neji."*

The small square of red in the row on the robot's metal chest ceased flashing. "You should have identified yourselves earlier, gentlemen." He bowed and stepped aside. "Go right on in."

"This is only," reminded Sands as he resumed climbing, "the first barrier."

The large reception foyer of the Pleasure Dome was thick with noise, music and people. Beautiful young women, naked to the waist, were circulating through the crowd with trays of snacks.

"Some of your biofoods?" asked Jake.

"As a matter of fact, no. Sonny gets the stuff from a cousin of his in Rio." Sands glanced around. "You should like the serving girls, though, since they're all andies that . . . Oof!"

"Trot on over to the nearest upramp," suggested Jake, after nudging him in the back with the lazgun.

On an airfloat dais that hovered five feet above the mosaic, neon-trimmed floor a quartet of bewigged chrome robots was playing greatly amplified Bach.

Beyond the foyer the wide, arched doorway to the dice and card pavilion showed.

"Look it up in the guidebook, Arlen," said a thin, blonde young woman who was pushing her way through the milling Dome customers at the side of a tuxed black man.

"I already know it's on Level 2, Charmaine."

"Then that's where we go first. I'm determined to see at least one DeathWrestling match before we leave Acapulco."

"We're moving a mite slowly," Jake said. "Nudge more assertively, Sands."

"Sonny does such excellent business here that the establishment is always crowded," said Sands over his shoulder. "Are you sure you wish to hurry this—since more than likely these are your last moments on Earth?"

Eventually they reached an automatic ramp. It carried them smoothly and quietly up to the next level of the Dome.

They skirted the packed rows of seats in the racing vidroom, where customers were watching and betting on horse races from all over the globe.

A lovely Chinese girl in a plasleather dress suddenly jumped up out of her red-plush chair. "Get this blinking thing off me!" she cried, swatting at the bloody, bedraggled bird that had just landed in her trim lap.

"One of the roosters from the cockfight lounge," explained Sands with a faint smile. "The little devils get away from time to time."

A small, polite silver robot went rushing over to the screaming, flapping young woman. He grabbed the squawking rooster and deftly wrung its neck.

"Something similar is going to happen to you, Cardigan."

"Onward and upward," Jake advised.

The next ramp transported them up to the third level and the soft-lit reception area for one of the bordellos. An efficient young woman behind an antique 20th Century metal desk looked up and inquired, "Do you prefer android or human companions, gentlemen—male or female?"

"We're just passing through, ma'am," explained Jake amiably. "Head for that ramp yonder, Sands."

"You know, Cardigan, I think you're actually doing all this just to get back at me for sleeping with your wife."

"I'm doing this because I'm being paid to find Kittridge and his daughter."

"Perhaps. Didn't you actually know about our earlier affair?"

Jake made no reply.

This ramp left them off in front of a blank gray door.

After making a faint whistling sound for five seconds, the door slid open. "Good evening again, Mr. Sands," said its voxbox. "We don't seem to have your companion on file. Would you mind identifying him for us?"

"Jake Cardigan," said Jake, urging Sands across the threshold and into the long, gray corridor beyond.

As the door rushed shut behind them, another opened at the far end of the corridor.

Two men appeared, both of them large and one a cyborg with each of his arms made of gunmetal.

"A bit of trouble, Mr. Sands?" inquired the cyborg.

"Only for Mr. Cardigan here."

Jake said, "We're here to see Sonny Hokori."

Sands added, "Without an appointment."

"If your buddy'll put down the gun," said the cyborg, "we can maybe see about—"

"Explain to them," suggested Jake as he prodded Sands with the barrel of the lazgun, "about how impatient and easily annoyed I am tonight."

"We'd best see Sonny," said Sands.

A third man appeared in the doorway. He was plump, about thirty-five and Japanese. His suit was a silky black and had dozens of small golden birds in flight across its jacket. "I've been wanting to meet Cardigan for a heck of a long time," he said, smiling cordially. "Hiya, Jake. C'mon in."

"After your goons retreat."

Chuckling, Sonny Hokori nudged the cyborg. "Hear what Jake called ya, Leon? Apparently that nearly two years at Harvard didn't help ya much."

"Cardigan's fucking opinion of me doesn't—"

"You and Brew go wait in the rumpus room, Leon," suggested the smiling Japanese.

After glaring at Jake, rubbing the metal fingers of his left hand along the back of his right, the cyborg withdrew. The other man followed.

"Goons." Hokori chuckled, shook his head. "Ya can both come in now, Jake."

Hokori's office was large, its curved off-white walls covered with rows of vidscreens that monitored the goings-on in every sector of the Pleasure Dome. There was no desk, only a white armchair next to a bank of computer terminals.

Seating himself in the armchair, Hokori nodded toward a nearby sofa. "Ya can share that, guys," he said. "Jake Cardigan. Jake Cardigan. Ya realize how many years our effing lives have been intertwined—and yet we've never met face to face. Funny. Life can be funny as heck at times." Chuckling, he turned to Sands. "Asshole, I thought ya told me ya were smarter than Cardigan."

"I've still no reason, Sonny, to believe I'm not."

Still standing, Jake said, "Here's what I have in mind, Hokori. If you don't have Kittridge and his daughter here in this office within five minutes—I'll start using this lazgun. First on Sands, then on you."

The Tek lord chuckled. "I tell ya, Jake, the way I feel about this asshole right about now, you could slice him up into sixteen mismatched chunks and I wouldn't give a darn," he said. "My own person I'm somewhat fonder of."

"Order the Kittridges brought here."

"Were I planning to go along with ya, Jake, I could only produce the prof," said Hokori. "But that feisty daughter of his—"

Just then five of the wall screens started flashing red. A loud hooting filled the big office.

The five screens were flashing new pictures now. Of unmarked skycruisers hovering around the Dome out there in the misty night.

The hooting was joined by siren wails.

Then most of the far wall of Hokori's office began to glow an intense sizzling orange. In less than ten seconds the whole stretch of wall turned to gray, gritty dust and fell away into the fog outside.

One of the hovering black skycruisers had attached itself to the side of the Dome. Its nose fell open and four dark-clothed men carrying lazrifles came scrambling into the office through the wide, new gap in the wall.

Foremost in the charging wedge was Kurt Winterguild, the bald-headed Field Director of the International Drug Control Agency. There was a look of intense satisfaction on his deeply tanned face, and the single rosebud tattooed on his polished scalp glowed especially red.

While half of his office wall was still in the process of disintegrating, Sonny Hokori had, nimbly, somersaulted out of his chair and gone scurrying behind the bank of computer terminals.

As the quartet of raiding IDCA agents fanned out across his office, the plump Japanese popped briefly to his feet. He was clutching an ebony needle-gun.

A blast of thirty silver darts came spurting out of the weapon. Almost every one hit the agent to the left of Winterguild.

The lean blond man howled as he was carried back across the

gritty floor by the force of the metal darts stitching into his body.

Had the wall been intact, he'd have slammed into it. Since it was no longer there, however, he kept going. He fell out into the mist, screaming, twitching, blood throbbing out of his multitude of tiny wounds.

Before Hokori could duck back down, Winterguild had swung his lazrifle and fired.

The beam, quickly and efficiently, sliced the Tek lord's head clean off his body.

Meantime Jake had caught Sands's arm, hustling him toward the nearest doorway. "Where's Kittridge?"

"Through here." Sands slapped at the recog panel and the door slid away.

"Halt!" ordered an agent from across the room. "This is an official IDCA raid. Nobody leaves."

Dropping into a low crouch, Jake went diving through the freshly opened doorway.

Sands started to follow, but a lazrifle beam found him and cut off his left arm just above the elbow.

His keening screams of pain were cut off when the door shut behind Jake.

Gun in hand, he started, cautiously yet rapidly, along the pale, peach-colored corridor.

He'd covered about a hundred feet when a door on his right started to whisper open.

Jake halted, gun pointing.

A sleepy-eyed, redheaded young woman in a rumpled suit of polka-dot pajamas came shambling out into the hall. "What the fuck's going on?" she asked in a drowsy murmur.

"Trouble," he told her. "Just stay right there—don't try to run."

"Shit."

"Where are the Kittridges?"

"Who?"

"The professor."

"Oh." Dreamily, she raised her hand and pointed. "Second door down that way there. Where's Sonny?"

"Dead and gone."

"Shit."

Jake ran along the corridor. The second door was standing open, making uneasy clicking noises. Thick greenish smoke was rolling along the hallway beyond.

Taking a deep breath and holding it, Jake headed into the smoky corridor.

A thickset man came running at him out of the smoke, his clothes aflame, screaming. He passed right by Jake, staggering more and more, bumping into the walls.

Jake kept moving ahead.

There was a large rectangular room at the corridor's end. About half of its outer wall was gone. Another International Drug Control Agency skycruiser was attached to the Dome here, nose gaping open. Two agents, each carrying a lazgun, were standing over the thin man who was sprawled on his back near a cot.

It was Professor Kittridge.

Winterguild arrived before his two agents got around to shooting Jake.

They both had their lazguns trained on him, though, and the one who was as bald as his boss was saying, "Stand back away from the professor, mister."

"Did you halfwits kill him?"

"He's only out cold, conked on the head by a chunk of debris or something. But suppose you explain just who in the hell you—"

"My boy, you've been doing a lot better than I expected." Winterguild came strolling into the room, signaling his men to lower their weapons. "We had a considerable head start on you, yet you arrived just about simultaneously."

"Jesus, Kurt, why'd you pull a grandstanding raid like this? You practically burn the Dome down, kill Hokori before he can even be questioned and—"

"We're flamboyant, my boy, granted. But that's what you need to scare these bastards."

Jake knelt down next to the unconscious Professor Kittridge. "You nearly knocked off the professor, too. And Sands is probably dead by now, too."

"Sands is alive." Winterguild rubbed once at the rosebud tattooed on his skull with bloody fingers. "He was quite talkative before he passed out. Instructing my medics to withhold the painkillers until he decided to cooperate did the trick."

Jake asked him, "Where's Beth Kittridge?"

"Not here, alas."

Jake felt suddenly cold. "Did they kill her?"

"Not at all, my boy. The young lady managed to escape sometime yesterday."

"Yesterday? Did she get in touch with you—or with the local cops?"

"She contacted no one, and Sands had no notion of where she went."

Jake rose up. "If she got free yesterday—why didn't she get help for her father?"

"She's apparently unhappy with him, Jake."

Looking down at Professor Kittridge, Jake said, "So he was planning to sell out to Hokori?"

"Apparently so, according to Sands. That upset Miss Kittridge and she went into hiding."

"I'll have to find her."

"I'd rather you didn't try, my boy," suggested the IDCA man. "Kittridge, after all, has been located and is alive. Cosmos and its client should be gratified at that news."

"Job's not over until I locate them both." Turning away, Jake started for the door.

Snapping his fingers before he got there, he stopped and retraced his steps.

Grinning, he punched Winterguild square on the chin.

The bald man stumbled back three paces, rolling from side to side to maintain his balance. "It's all right, boys, don't shoot him."

"That's the one I promised you back at Spaceland Park," explained Jake and left.

He was awake when the robot came to get him.

Jake had finally returned to the hotel suite about an hour before dawn. Not turning any of the lights on, he'd stood at the wraparound window and watched the foggy city.

About the only thing he was able to get any satisfaction out of was the fact that he hadn't given in to the urge to use Tek again.

"Stuff's still damn tough for me to keep away from," he said aloud, slumping down into an armchair.

Actually he hadn't done that badly so far. He'd established that Kittridge was alive and he'd located him. That would make Bascom and the Cosmos Detective Agency happy.

"But there's still Beth," he said.

She was the one who was important, the one he had to find.

"She's dead," he said to himself.

"No, that was only an android simulacrum. A mechanism, not a person. Jake knew that, but it didn't seem to help what he felt.

He felt that Beth, someone he'd become very fond of, was lost to him.

Jake stayed in the chair, looking absently out into the dying night. Gradually he drifted into an uneasy sleep.

When he awoke the fog was gone. A thin sunlight touched the towers and walkways of Acapulco.

And Jake knew where to find Beth.

"She's gone to her uncle's villa," he said, getting up from the chair. "Sure, the place on the Moon that she told me about."

That would've been exactly what she'd do. She was deeply upset, not certain whom she could trust. She'd want to get away by herself, to be alone where nobody could contact her for a while.

"I've got to get there." Jake was striding toward the door of the suite when it opened itself.

"I was certain we'd be seeing each other soon again," said the chrome-plated Winger as he entered. "If you have a moment, Cardigan, I have to talk to you about a rather serious parole violation."

The chrome-plated robot brushed at the sleeve of his white suit, tugged carefully at his trouser legs and seated himself in the armchair. "Since I don't require rest," he explained to Jake, "I was ready to depart for Mexico the moment the complaint reached the Southern California Parole Authority. As I've all along anticipated, you're almost certain to return to the Freezer within—"

"I'm in the middle of something important," Jake told the gleaming robot. "I don't have time for you right now."

"I'm the one who has the time and you're going to have to accommodate me." Winger settled into the chair. "The Field Director of the International Drug Control Agency has filed a complaint against you. You should have realized, Cardigan, that when you assaulted an important law official, you were risking a serious violation."

Jake held up one finger. "I gave Winterguild one punch on the chin."

"Which constitutes a serious assault."

"As I recall the rules, Winger, you have to hold a formal hearing before you can charge me with a parole violation of any kind."

"And I'm in the process of gathering the material for that hearing right here and now," the robot informed him. "If you'll cooperate by sitting down, we can start this little preliminary discussion."

"Soon as I finish what I have to do," promised Jake, "we can have a nice long chat." He started toward the door.

"I'm not against using force to persuade you to stay," warned the robot as he stood.

Stopping and facing him, Jake said, "I have to find Beth Kittridge. I'm fairly certain where she is and—"

"You can tell me her present whereabouts and I'll see to it the information gets to Winterguild. He's also most anxious to locate her."

"Looks like you're going to have to try force," said Jake impatiently, "because I can't wait around here to—"

The door of the suite all at once opened itself again. Gomez came limping in, smiling broadly. Ignoring Jake, he addressed the immaculate robot. "Is this the room that just phoned for a repairman?"

"It isn't," snapped Winger, making a shooing motion with one chrome hand. "I happen to be conducting an official investigation for the government of the State of Southern California. Your intrusion is—"

"Hey, they told me there was a malfunctioning robot up here, *señor.*" With a slight limp, Gomez made his way into the living room of the suite.

"You've been misinformed. There's no malfunctioning robot here."

"Ah, but there's where you're wrong, *amigo.*" Smiling, Gomez suddenly reached up to touch the mechanical man's silvery neck. A harsh buzzing sound came from something concealed in his hand.

Winger's eyelids started blinking in double time. "You used a disabler on me . . . that's most illegal . . ." Both hands dropped heavily to his sides, his eyes clicked shut and he ceased to function.

Gomez was in the pilot seat of the maroon and yellow skycar. "You may commence at any time, *amigo,* heaping gratitude on me."

"Assaulting a robot can be a serious crime. I appreciate your helping out, but—"

"The particular disabler I used to render Winger even stiffer than usual," said his partner, "has a wipe-out attachment. It erased all his chrome-plated memories back ten full minutes before my auspicious advent."

Nodding, Jake said, "How'd you know he was coming to call on me?"

"The Cosmos Agency specializes in gathering little tidbits of information from hither and yon. And from yon came the news that that putz Winterguild had complained to the parole folks because you'd tipped him over onto his toke."

"One punch."

"Sufficient to inspire him to have you rerouted back to the Freezer."

"So Winger hinted when he dropped in on me."

"However, even as we speak, even as you drink in my words of wisdom delivered in the melodious voice that has been known to charm birds out of trees and both princesses and bimbos into the sack—where was I?"

"I hope you were going to make a point about my being able to keep clear of the damn Freezer."

"Exactly, *amigo.* Bascom's pulling the usual strings to derail, circumvent and otherwise circumlocute the complaint." Gomez glanced down at Acapulco below. "Ah, we're fast approaching our destination. The only snag is that it'll take Bascom at least a full working day to get everything canceled. I decided, therefore, to pop down here to the country of my illustrious ancestors to roadblock Winger before he could do you any harm. *Entiendes?*"

"Yeah, and thanks."

"It's *nada,*" Gomez assured him. "I think nothing of dragging my pain-racked body out of my sickbed and hobbling to your assistance, Jake, thereby denying myself the ministrations of three gifted physicians, seven medbots and five fetching nurses—two of whom seem to be named Mitzi."

"About this private spaceport we're heading for?"

"Owned and operated by a contact of mine." Gomez punched out a landing pattern. "If we want to make a quick jaunt up to the Moon without anyone being the wiser, Montanya is the gent who can arrange it all."

"We?"

"*Sí,* of course," said Gomez, smiling. "I don't want to miss out on the close of this case."

After nearly half an hour in the communications room at the edge of the small spaceport, Jake pushed back the metal chair he was sitting in. Looking away from the computer terminal, he glanced up at the vidporn calendar on the opposite wall. On the small screen Miss April was about to jump into bed with two husky skysailors.

Jake left the chair, and the view of the animated calendar, to start pacing the room.

There was a tap on the door, followed by the entrance of Gomez. "All the details have been smoothly and swiftly taken care of, Jake," he announced, noticing the calendar on the wall. "I didn't know anybody wore those anymore. . . . Ah, but back to reality. We're the proud temporary owners of a trim mooncraft, booked to blast off in exactly two hours and sixteen minutes."

"How'd you arrange such a quick departure?"

Gomez smiled. "Montanya owes me a few favors," he replied, resting a hand atop a terminal. "I trust you won't mind that our bark on this fateful journey has MOONBASE GOURMET FOOD SHOPS, LTD. emblazoned on several portions of its exterior. It helps our cover story, actually."

Jake said, "Thanks to your buddy's somewhat unorthodox information-gathering setup here, I've been able to check on all the Moon flights that Beth Kittridge might've been on."

"And?"

"Well, nobody by that name departed anywhere in Mexico—not on a Moonliner, a tourship or a private charter."

"It figures she wouldn't use her true name or ID papers."

"But there are two possible passengers to the Moon who could be her," he told his partner, "one of whom listed her name as Bev Kingsmill."

"Oy, she's not the sort who keeps her initials when she adopts an alias, is she?"

"She struck me as brighter than that, but I won't rule this lady out."

"So what you've concluded, *amigo,* is that it is indeed possible she's holed up on the Moon?"

"Yeah, especially since no one closely resembling her seems to have used any public means of transport out of Acapulco since the time Beth escaped from the Pleasure Dome—that includes skyliners, landbuses and rented skycars."

"Then," said Gomez, pointing upward, "we may as well go to the Moon."

When Jake came walking into the galley of their Moonbound spacecraft, Gomez was arguing with the kitchen computer.

His curly-haired partner was sitting slightly hunched in front of the terminal inset in the gray wall next to the stove unit. He had a plaschina bowl in his left hand and was gesturing with the spoon in his right. "How can you have gone wrong on oatmeal?" he was asking. "It's one of the basics of the human diet, has been for countless centuries."

"Well, let's give her another try," said the terminal's voxbox. "How about the raisins—they taste okay?"

Gomez set the bowl on a gray counter and kept the spoon. "*Sí*, but I'd like them some other color than blue this time."

Jake sat at the gray-metal galley dining table. "I got through to the Cosmos Agency again on the satphone."

"Since you look somewhat less gloomy and morose than you have during the past eighteen hours of our jaunt through the vast wilderness of space," he said, gesturing at the clear darkness outside the viewport, "I'd guess Bascom had some relatively good news."

Jake said, "He did, yeah. Bascom's been able to get my parole-violation charges dropped. So at least I won't be heading back to the Freezer."

"Let this be a lesson to you. You're going to have to be much more selective in the future about which assholes you knock down and where." Gomez eyed the stove. "What about getting the old charges against you wiped out entirely? Since we ought to be able to prove now that Sands and Hokori framed you back then."

"Sands is still in a coma, so that's going to have to wait."

"What about the fate of your one-time missus?"

"Kate's cooperating with the various lawmen. Looks like she won't be charged with anything."

"And where's Dan?"

"He's still at that private school in Mexico City. When I get back, I'm going to have to work a few things out with Kate. I want to be involved in my son's life again."

"Sounds like the lad could use that about now." Gomez waved at the stove with his spoon. "Oatmeal?"

"Coming up," promised the terminal. "We want to make sure we get it absolutely right this time."

Gomez joined Jake at the table. "Okay, next I'll ask an unpleasant question—do you think Kate was in on your original frame-up?"

Putting both of his hands palmsdown on the metal tabletop, Jake said, "I don't know, I don't have enough facts yet."

"What about your cop instincts? Do they tell you anything?"

"Maybe I'm ignoring my intuitive feelings," admitted Jake. "It's going to take awhile to sort all this out. Some of it's going to depend on what Sands has to say when—and if—he wakes up again."

"Wait'll you've had a few more wives, *amigo.* It'll be a lot easier to accept that one of them may've done you wrong," Gomez assured him. "How about Professor Kittridge—what's his version of recent events?"

"According to our boss, Kittridge is claiming he was kidnapped, he and his daughter. Says he had no idea that Sands was a partner of Hokori's."

"With Sands in slumberland and Hokori among the angels," said Gomez, "that's hard to refute. Thing is, Beth allegedly took off because she realized her dear old dad was intending to sell out to the forces of evil."

"That's another reason why I want to find Beth."

"She may decide to act the way you're acting about Kate—and simply back off from the whole problem."

"Everybody does that sometimes, Sid. Turns out I've been backing off from problems for the past fifteen years."

Gomez put up both hands, as though fending off a charge. "Whoa, now," he cautioned. "This is commencing to get dangerously close to a serious conversation on the meaning of life and how we perceive it. I don't like to dwell on my true purpose for existing, beyond admitting that I was put on Earth to gladden the hearts of the multitudes."

Managing a grin, Jake said, "One thing I am sure of—I want to keep working for the Cosmos Agency."

"*Sí,* it would be a shame to split up the team again. And I really will strive not to break a limb every time out."

"Oatmeal's ready," announced the terminal in a pleased tone.

They docked at the landing dome of New Moonbase II thirty-seven hours after leaving Earth. Outside the milky seethru walls of the great dome, two other similar domes showed. Beyond that spread the white, silent desolation of the Moon itself.

"Reminds me of some real estate I once invested in around the Palm Springs Sector," observed Gomez as he disembarked from their anchored spacecraft. "Except my quarter acre sported a cactus."

"She'll be here," said Jake, mostly to himself, following his partner onto a downramp that led to the Customs Complex. The artificial air inside the dome felt harsh on his throat and in his lungs. He coughed.

"Ah, *amigo,* you miss the pollution-scented air of our old hometown." The ramp took them to an entryway for the first below-surface level of the Moon Colony. "Allow me to take care of the customs folks."

There were two white-enameled robots seated at the silvery desk beneath the floating COMMERCIAL VEHICLES sign.

Gomez introduced himself as a spacetrucker for the Moonbase Gourmet Food Shops, Ltd., organization. He produced spurious ID papers for himself and Jake, plus all the proper bills of lading, unloading permits and travel visas. The whole process took a little over seven minutes and both the robots, almost in unison, wished Gomez and Jake a pleasant sojourn on the Moon.

Three minutes later they were in a subway car heading for the Old Settlement. The twenty-four-seat car was chill and clean and they were the only passengers. Six silent vidcommercials played on the row of large screens on the left-hand side of the compartment. Two of the ads were for Sands food products.

Jake coughed again. "Old Settlement's about thirty miles from here," he said. "Beth's uncle has his villa down on OS/Level 2."

Through the windows on their right showed the dead-white walls of the tunnel the subway train was rushing through.

"You're absolutely and totally certain," inquired his partner, "that you want to encounter the authentic Beth Kittridge in person?"

"Yeah—I have to," answered Jake. "It's what I've been moving toward since I got out of the Freezer."

"This Beth may not be a ringer for the android version."

"She'll be close."

Gomez laughed quietly. "Hey, you really did—really did fall in love."

"I came to like her a hell of a lot. And I want to see her again."

"Except that this Beth, the original, doesn't know about that. Fact is, she doesn't even know you at all."

"I'm going to have to risk that," acknowledged Jake with a quick nod. "I'm pretty sure I dreamed about her, in the Freezer, just before they woke me up." He stared out at the bright-lit white walls that went flashing by. "I don't know why—I must've seen Beth before somewhere—maybe it was a premonition. Then you came around to show me a picture of her, and next Bascom showed me a hologram in his office. Finally I met the android duplicate."

"Obviously you have to meet the real Beth Kittridge," agreed Gomez. "That's the last move in the game."

"Okay, I know it sounds a mite odd. Keep in mind, though, that it also ends this assignment."

"It maybe ends the assignment so far as Bascom and Cosmos are concerned," he said. "But you're going to have a few loose ends of your own to tie up. That, *amigo,* may take you a considerable while to do."

The villa was nearly a mile from the final stop of the OS/Level 2 subway line. Jake walked from the small, run-down station alone. Gomez told him he preferred to wait on the station's one remaining bench, since sentimental reunions made him uncomfortably tearful.

The other estates down on this level were real, but most of the trees, grass and shrubbery were hologram projections. The whole system was no longer in great shape, and every so often all the trees would grow dim and then vanish completely for a few seconds, along with all the flowers and all the vast lawns, leaving only metal flooring showing. The area was in its night cycle; the wide, tree-lined streets were dark. Less than half the floating streetlamps were functioning; lights showed at the windows of only two of the houses he passed.

On the vast appearing and disappearing lawn of one of the villas a robot gardener was pretending to be pruning the shrubs. "Howdy, friend," he called as Jake went by.

"Evening."

"Howdy, friend. Howdy, friend . . ."

There were lights showing in the villa he'd come to visit. Just inside the open, rusted iron gates stood a mechanical guard dog. One of its plasglass eyes had fallen out, its imitation fur was patchy and it could manage nothing more than a very weak growl when Jake entered the grounds.

The air down here must be thinner than it was up in the dome. Jake was having trouble with his breathing.

Coughing again, he hurried up to the villa along its simulated path, climbed the five steps to knock on the authentic oaken door.

After nearly a half minute he heard shuffling footsteps from inside. In another half minute the door opened a few inches. "What . . . what . . . what do you wish, sir?" A very ancient robot butler, his silvery head tarnished, his dark suit frayed, appeared in the opening.

"My name's Jake Cardigan. I'm an operative with the Cosmos Detective Agency in Greater Los Angeles," he said. "I'd like to see Miss Kittridge."

"I'm . . . I'm not certain that's possible. Allow . . . allow me to determine if Miss Kittridge is . . . is receiving visitors this evening." He started to shut the door and turn away.

Jake gently nudged the door wider open with his foot. He stepped across the threshold and into the shadowy foyer.

"It's all right, Edward." She was standing on a low step of the wide, curving staircase. She held a lazgun pointed at Jake. "I'm Beth Kittridge."

It was Beth. Alive again and looking exactly as she had the last time he'd been with her. "I was hired to find you by your insurance company," he explained, moving nearer to her. "I thought you might be here. Quite a few things have happened since you left Acapulco, and it's safe to come home now."

The frown faded from her face and she took a few steps toward him. "Jake Cardigan," she said slowly and thoughtfully. "Yes, my father—when I still had faith in him—spoke highly of you. Your record as a cop wasn't all that admirable toward the end, but we concluded you'd been framed." She nodded, smiling quietly at him. "Yes, I think I can trust you."

"You can, yeah."

She lowered the gun to her side, moving even closer to him. "You know," she said, "I have the feeling we've met somewhere before."

Jake grinned at her. "Matter of fact, we have," he said. "Let me tell you about it."